LYNN KURLAND

A WINTER'S MAGIC

NOVELLAS OF THE NINE KINGDOMS

Praise for
the Novels of the Nine Kingdoms

River of Dreams

"Elegant writing . . . An enchanting, vibrant story that captures romance, fantasy, and adventure with intriguing detail and an epic, fairy-tale sensibility." —*Kirkus Reviews*

"Aisling and Rùnach's tender romance sweetly ratchets up as they take turns saving each other from perilous danger, and series fans will be left eager to read about their future adventures."
—*Publishers Weekly*

"Fantastic . . . As always, the world building is rich and vivid and the characters fascinating and well-rounded, which is why Kurland's books are truly awesome reads!" —*RT Book Reviews* (Top Pick)

"Time after time, book after book, Lynn Kurland crafts a tale vividly alive with imagination . . . She weaves stories with a magic that could only be conjured from dreams." —*The Reading Cafe*

Dreamspinner

"Fascinating, well-drawn characters and vibrant descriptions of magical situations and locations reinforce a vivid, enchanting narrative." —*Kirkus Reviews*

"The writing is classic Lynn Kurland—fluid and graceful."
—*The Romance Reader*

"Awe-inspiring . . . The beginning of a new quest that will be filled with ample quantities of adventure, magic and peril!"
—*RT Book Reviews*

"Lyrical writing, brilliant mental imagery, richly descriptive magic, and larger than life characterization." —*The Reading Cafe*

Gift of Magic

"The exciting story line is fast-paced from the onset . . . Lynn Kurland spins another fabulous fantasy." —*Genre Go Round Reviews*

"A magical combination of action, fantasy, and character exploration that is truly wonderful! A journey well worth taking!"
—*RT Book Reviews*

Spellweaver

"One of the strongest fantasy novels welcoming in the new year."
—*Fresh Fiction*

"Kurland weaves together intricate layers of plot threads, giving this novel a rich and lyrical style." —*RT Book Reviews*

A Tapestry of Spells

"Kurland deftly mixes innocent romance with adventure in a tale that will leave readers eager for the next installment."
—*Publishers Weekly*

"Captured my interest from the very first page." —*Night Owl Reviews*

Princess of the Sword

"Beautifully written, with an intricately detailed society born of Ms. Kurland's remarkable imagination." —*Romance Reviews Today*

"An intelligent, involving tale full of love and adventure."
—*All About Romance*

Titles by Lynn Kurland

STARDUST OF YESTERDAY

A DANCE THROUGH TIME

THIS IS ALL I ASK

THE VERY THOUGHT OF YOU

ANOTHER CHANCE TO DREAM

THE MORE I SEE YOU

IF I HAD YOU

MY HEART STOOD STILL

FROM THIS MOMENT ON

A GARDEN IN THE RAIN

DREAMS OF STARDUST

MUCH ADO IN THE MOONLIGHT

WHEN I FALL IN LOVE

WITH EVERY BREATH

TILL THERE WAS YOU

ONE ENCHANTED EVENING

ONE MAGIC MOMENT

ALL FOR YOU

ROSES IN MOONLIGHT

DREAMS OF LILACS

STARS IN YOUR EYES

EVER MY LOVE

A LOVELY DAY TOMORROW

The Novels of the Nine Kingdoms

STAR OF THE MORNING

THE MAGE'S DAUGHTER

PRINCESS OF THE SWORD

A TAPESTRY OF SPELLS

SPELLWEAVER

GIFT OF MAGIC

DREAMSPINNER

RIVER OF DREAMS

DREAMER'S DAUGHTER

THE WHITE SPELL

THE DREAMER'S SONG

THE PRINCE OF SOULS

Anthologies

Love Came Just in Time

A Winter's Magic (Nine Kingdoms)

eSpecials

"To Kiss in the Shadows" from Tapestry

A Winter's Magic
Copyright © 2023 by Kurland Book Productions, Inc.

Kurland Book
Productions

First Edition: 2023

Print ISBN: 978-1-961496-00-2
eBook ISBN: 978-1-961496-01-9

Cover and Formatting: Streetlight Graphics
Map Art: Tara Larsen Chang

This is a work of fiction. Names, characters, places, and incidents either are the product of the author's imagination or are used fictitiously, and any resemblance to locales, events, business establishments, or actual persons—living or dead—is entirely coincidental.

Dear Friends,

I'm so pleased to be able to offer this reissue of two Nine Kingdoms novellas that have been gathering dust for far too long.

Harold of Neroche wants nothing more than a decent adventure, but the weather outside is foul and no one seems particularly interested in stirring up mischief inside. He settles for his father reading A Tale of Two Swords, which recounts the adventures of a pair who might turn out to be a bit more involved in Harry's life than he ever could have imagined.

In A Whisper of Spring, we take a journey back in time to meet Simon, the first king of Neroche. He's taken up residence in his father's hunting lodge where he suspects his evenings will contain nothing more interesting than watching his hounds dreaming of the chase before the fire. All that changes in an instant when a banished elf walks in, uninvited and unexpected, and demands Symon rescue his sister who has been carried off by the evil mage keeping house just across their northern border. Symon accepts the quest . . . and also decides that no one needs to know how long he's worshipped Iolaire of Ainneamh—or how much he's willing to gamble to not only save her life, but have her heart.

I hope you'll enjoy these peeks into the early history of the Nine Kingdoms. There will definitely be more to come!

Happy reading!
Lynn

The Nine Kingdoms

Wychweald

·Riamh

Aigeann
Sea

Jor
Neroche

Diarmailt

Penrhyn

·Well

Neroche

Ain—

·Chagailt   Gilean·

Gobhann·

·Bère

Angesand·

Lismór
·

Melksham
Island

·Istaur

M. I.

Bay of
Sonasach

·Sonasach

Diore

Meith

Shettlestoune

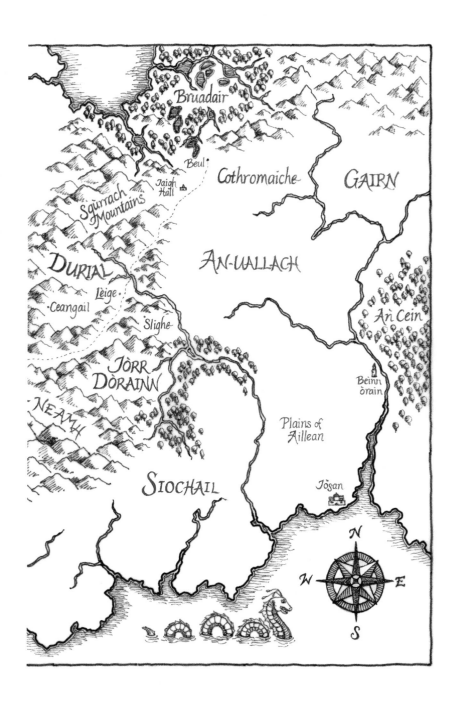

The Tale of Two Swords

Prologue

Harold needed an adventure.

He rolled over onto his belly and contemplated the potential for such a thing. All the elements necessary for the planning of an important quest were about him: foul weather outside; a hot fire inside; his own enthusiasm for the idea at a fever pitch; and the luxury of planning his scheme in a cozy chamber in what was otherwise a very drafty castle.

Now, if he had been a man of five-and-twenty, well-armored, well-horsed, and well-trained in the arts of war, he might have commanded the adventure himself. Unfortunately, he was just an eight-year-old boy who found himself quite generally being swept out from underfoot by those more suited to the doing of mighty deeds than he. But he was a clever lad, so his age would not be a detriment to his ambitions.

He looked at his brother, Reynauld, a supremely focused but otherwise unimaginative lad of ten-and-five who currently studied a complicated battlefield peopled with wooden warriors not of his own making.

Nay, Harold decided, there would be no aid from that quarter.

He looked at his sister, Imogen, a beautiful, dreamy girl of twelve summers who loved lavish fabrics and abhorred dirt of all kinds. Imogen's idea of a good adventure was limited to pressing him and his grubby self into service as a mannequin so she might see how an endless array of itchy materials might grace her slight shoulders. Harold knew that asking her to cast her lot in with him would entail a repayment of hours spent doing just that kind of wearisome labor, and there were some things that even he would not do for the sake of a noble quest. He would have to look elsewhere.

He turned his piercing gaze upon his mother. She sat in a chair near him, fashioning some sort of needlework. He stared at her hands and felt warmth rush into his heart. He suspected it wasn't a manly thing to admit—that he loved his mother's hands—so he kept the sentiment locked inside his heart where he could examine it privately. Serving, creating, soothing; his mother's hands were never still. He liked the soothing best, but that was another unmanly sentiment he would never admit to unless death loomed.

Not that his mother's hands were limited to those gentler arts. He had, on one glorious occasion earlier that winter, seen his mother snatch up a fire iron and impale an enormous spider with it. If he hadn't known better, he would have sworn his mother looked as skilled with a poker as any member of the king's guard was with a sword—not that he'd ever seen a member of the king's guard, mind you, but he could imagine their skill quite well. It had been a deed worthy of song, that one.

He stroked his chin thoughtfully. (He did that often. He was certain it made him look wise beyond his years.) *Had* his mother more skills than she let on? Those thin white scars she bore on her hands; could those have come from learning to use a sword?

He paused.

He considered.

Then he shook his head. Impossible. This was his mother, after all, and as jolly a fellow as he considered her to be, the thought of her hefting a sword and tramping about in the mud to master its use was simply too far beyond even the vast reaches of his formidable imagination for serious contemplation. Her scars had likely come from the innumerable things she did to keep their household with its small battalion of servants, not to mention the secret messengers his father received at all hours that Harold wasn't supposed to know about, in top form.

But in spite of the origin of her scars, and because of her love for him, he knew he could count on her to aid him in whatever business he might be about. She had done it often enough in the past.

She had also been up half the night tending him whilst he puked his guts out in various pots, so perhaps he should give her a rest for the day.

He turned to his sire. Here were riper pickings.

"Father," he said, sitting up and using his most polite tone, "would you have a mind for an adventure?"

His father slowly lowered the missive he'd been reading, blinked a time or two at Harold as if he weren't quite seeing him, then frowned. "Hmmm?"

"An adventure, Father."

"An adventure? In the snow?"

Harold suspected that if his sire looked that unwilling to tramp about outside in a blizzard, then he likely wouldn't be interested in tramping about inside, either. Obviously, a compromise would have to be made.

"A story, then," Harold said, thinking quickly. If he couldn't live out his own epic compilation of events, then he would hear about someone else's and be content. "Bloodshed... great daring... aye, I have it. *The Tale of the Two Swords.*"

Reynauld groaned loudly. "Nay, not that. Too much romance."

"I like romance," Imogen said quickly. "Aye, Father, that one."

"*The Two Swords,*" their father said thoughtfully. "Very well, if you like." He rose and fetched a very well-used leather-bound volume from a shelf. "*The Two Swords,*" he muttered as he sat and gingerly turned the yellowing sheaves of parchment. "Aye, here it is. Now,

Harold," he said, looking over the top of the book at him, "where shall I start? With bloodshed? Mayhem? Long marches in the dead of night through marshy wastes infested with bugs of uncommonly potent stings?"

"Bloodshed," Reynauld said absently, moving his cavalry to a more advantageous locale.

"Romance," Imogen said with a dreamy sigh. "I like those parts—"

"Nay, begin where she flees the castle on one of Angesand's finest steeds," Reynauld interrupted. "There's a goodly bit of excitement there." He looked up at his sire. "And Angesand *does* produce the finest horses, Father."

"Aye, son, he does," their sire agreed. "Harold, have you an opinion on where we should begin?"

"Any time during those first few days of her harrowing escape would suit me, Father," Harold said obligingly.

"As you will, then." He cleared his throat, then began. "This chapter is entitled 'How Mehar of Angesand Escaped Her Father's Keep and Earned His Bounty on Her Head in One Night.'"

Harold settled himself more comfortably on the rug, placed his toes a bit closer to the fire, and smiled. Could his evening improve?

He doubted it.

Chapter One

In which Mehar of Angesand Escapes Her Father's Keep
and Earns His Bounty on Her Head in One Night...

T hunder rolled in the distance, driving before it an unwholesome
air.

In answer, the great horse gathered itself onto its haunches and
leapt up and over the upturned faces of half a dozen astonished
peasants who lingered at the mouth of the only visible track into a
densely populated bit of forest.

Mehar flattened herself against Fleet's back as he flew, lest she
find herself becoming too acquainted with any of the stray branches
that brushed past her. The last time Fleet had taken such a mighty
leap, it had been over a dozen of Angesand's gate guards, but then
it had been the rapidly lowering portcullis to catch at her, not the
branch of a tree. If she hadn't managed to free the catch of her
cloak, she would have surely been pulled backwards off her horse
and sent sprawling onto the cobblestones. But luck had been with
her that night; she had left her coat and her prison behind and galloped madly down the road.

There was no chance for such speed now. All she could do was
plunge her mount farther into the underbrush, then turn and whis-

per the one feeble spell she had at her command and hope it would do.

The air began to pulse against her ears, as if some strong wind behind it pushed it relentlessly on. The feeling of tension increased and with it the thunder until both turned into a company of horsemen who galloped up the road toward her hiding place. Leaves and peasants alike scattered before them.

She thought she had ridden hard.

Apparently, her father had ridden harder.

She held her breath as the company halted, then regrouped directly before her. She didn't dare try to escape. She might have outridden her sire and his men, but then again, she might not have, and that didn't bear thinking on. All she could do was hope that her spell would hold. She was no mage, she was a weaver, and she suspected the spell of un-noticing she'd woven about herself and Fleet might be nothing more than words hopefully spoken but yielding nothing of substance.

Damn her sire. Could he not have found a convenient tavern to loiter in and thereby save himself from the rain? Another pair of days would have served her well. Though she supposed the fact that she'd even come this far wasn't far short of a miracle.

That miracle she owed to the steed beneath her who had flown as if on wings. Her father had never produced his like before and likely never would again. Much the same could have been said about her, but no doubt in far less inspired tones of awe and admiration.

She scowled at Fleet's equine cousins who bore the company of men before her. A pity they hadn't done a bit of loitering as well. They had followed Fleet at first, given that she had liberated them from her father's stables along with Fleet, but they'd been no match for his speed. She had known her father would catch his horses soon enough, but she'd intended that even once he did, he would find no gear to put on them. The bridles, saddles, and other pertinent items in the stables had worn a spell of un-noticing that had been guaranteed to last at least two full days.

Then again, the mage who had taught her the spell hadn't been all that sure of the wording, and the times she'd tried to weave the spell over her sisters' things she hadn't been all that successful, but considering how attached her sisters were to their combs, beautifying herbs, and steel implements made to mold noses into pleasing shapes during sleep, it was difficult to determine if the spell had worked or not.

It was also hard to imagine her father being more intent on finding his gear than his daughters had been, but there you had it.

All of which left her standing where she was, under a dripping tree, watching the men before her and trying not to sneeze.

"My lord," one of the horsemen said carefully, "surely we have searched long enough—"

"Silence, Peter, you fool," Robert of Angesand barked. "It will be enough when we find that... that..." His fury obviously burned brightly even now. "I vow I'll kill her for this! Damn her for the trouble she's caused me!"

Mehar wondered what irritated him more: the inconvenience of having had to catch his horses or the embarrassment of not having had the goods to deliver to a wooing Prince of Hagoth.

"But, my lord," Peter said, aghast, "surely you don't mean—"

"I mean to hunt until I find her," Robert snarled. "And if I don't find her, I'll put a price on her head that a hundred hunters couldn't resist—if it beggars me to do it!"

Damn that Hagoth. Couldn't he have turned his clouded eye elsewhere? She had three quite serviceable sisters of marriageable age and tractable mien. Surely the dotard could have found one of them more suitable to his purposes than she.

He finds you... pretty. Her father had choked on that last word when he'd spewed it at her. He'd washed the taste of it out of his mouth with a hefty tankard of ale taken in one long, slow draught.

She wasn't pretty; she knew it. Her fingers were stained from dye, her skin tough from carding and spinning, and her hair (piled haphazardly on her head usually) and her clothes (piled haphazardly on her person always) left her looking more like a scullery maid than a lord's daughter. But she had sisters aplenty for wedding off to make alliances, which should have left her free to dress like a beggar and weave miracles.

It had, for quite some time. Until the Prince of Hagoth had taken one look at her and decided she was a filly begging to be broken to his brutal hand.

"In truth, I don't know why Hagoth would want her," Robert grumbled. "She's too much like her dam. Fey wench."

"Elfine had many gifts," Peter said quietly. "She wove beautiful things for your hall and your guests."

Mehar half expected her sire to run his captain through. Instead, he merely snorted. "You were half in love with her yourself, you fool," he said contemptuously. "I should have let you have her, her with her endless weaving and muttering and scribbling in that bloody book of hers." He paused. "I wonder what became of that?"

Mehar put her hand to her breast where that small book safely resided. It was the one thing of her mother's she'd managed to save when her sire had destroyed all her possessions in an effort to convince her that Hagoth truly was the man for her.

"Never should have let the wench take up her dam's work," her sire continued darkly. "I should have burned El—" He cursed, which was his usual alternative to saying his dead wife's name. "I should have burned the woman's gear the moment she drew her last."

At least he hadn't and for that, at least, Mehar was grateful. She'd had a dozen years to enjoy creating her own magic with her mother's tools. And she'd had a like number of years to puzzle over the small book her mother had kept ever near her.

A traveling mage, the one who had taught her the spell of unnoticing in return for a cloak, had said the book contained spells, but they weren't ones he could read. The wizard who had written them down for her mother would be the one who could, he had said. The king's finest court mage might be another, he had offered. Then he'd said that given the ease with which she'd learned his spell, perhaps one day she might be able to read the book. But a simple man such as himself? Nay, it was far beyond his art.

Mehar had considered his words long after he'd gone. She was quite certain no wizard had written her mother's book. The characters were in her mother's fine hand. She hadn't dared ask her sire about it. She'd been content to allow him to focus his attentions on her three younger, more beautiful, more empty-headed sisters and leave her to losing herself in the feel, the smell, and the work of her hands.

Of course, that had been before Hagoth had decided she was to be his, before her father had destroyed all her mother's weaving tools, before she had decided that flight was her only choice. Pulling away the cloak of mystery covering her mother's book had seemed like a fine idea as she'd freed herself from her bedchamber by clouting the guardsman outside over the head with a leg from her mother's ruined spinning wheel. Fleeing to the king's palace had seemed an even more brilliant plan as she'd silently slipped down the stairs and out through the kitchens whilst her father and the Prince of Hagoth were drinking themselves into insensitivity at her father's table. Remaking herself into a powerful mage had seemed the best plan of all as she'd raced down the road on her father's finest steed as if she really were in great haste to be about starting her future.

This all assumed, of course, that a court mage would help her, that she would find the king's palace in spite of the magic that was rumored to protect it, and, most pressingly, that she might keep her throat free of her father's clutching fingers long enough to search.

Back on the road in front of her, her father was vowing several more black oaths. He topped even himself as he contemplated aloud a proper reward for her head (attached or not), before he called his company to turn around and head back down the road to that inn they'd recently passed where he had damn well better find something strengthening before he decided upon a final price. Mehar had little trouble imagining how the rest of her father's se'nnight would go.

He would retreat to Angesand, call for every bounty hunter in the land, offer them a ridiculous sum for the doing of the deed, then try to bargain with them before they exited the hall. After that, he would sit about and curse them as weak-stomached fools who couldn't track a feeble wench for the sport of it and if he were younger, he would do it himself, but what with his stables to attend to and three other daughters to see properly married, and also the Prince of Hagoth to see appeased...

And all that would lead him back to wanting to kill her and then he might up the price a bit until there actually might be a fool who would think it worth his time.

It would behoove her to make haste whilst her father fingered the coins in his purse, bemoaning their scarcity.

Mehar swung up onto Fleet's back and turned him deeper into the forest. They would take the road again in another day or so, when she felt it was safe. But for now, with apologies to her mount, she drove him farther into the darkness of the thick undergrowth.

I t was hunger that almost undid her, hunger and a desperate need for warmth. After ten days, she had long since exhausted what little food she had brought with her. She had tried to forage for food, but she wasn't a hunter, and she hadn't dared make a fire to cook anything she might have caught.

At least she'd had no sightings of her sire, nor heard anyone making the stomping noises a tracker makes whilst hunting game he knows is far too simple-minded to realize it is being stalked.

She smelled a rabbit, nicely toasted, before she saw the fire. She pulled Fleet up quickly and hoped she hadn't been heard. The fire was built in a little clearing not far from where she could see the road ahead. A man sat there, examining the meal on the end of his stick, but he didn't look overly dangerous and she supposed she wouldn't have cared if he had been. She dug about in her purse, then spurred Fleet on. She burst through the trees and flung one of her precious coins at the man, who gaped at her as he fumbled for it. His spit went up into the air and she snatched it on her way by.

She left the forest behind her and thundered down the road.

It was only then she realized that her breakfast was hot as hell-fire.

She almost lost her seat *and* her meal, but she managed to get her skirts up and around the hare without finding herself sprawled in the dirt. Her hand burned, but it burned far less than her belly gnawed, so she ate and was very glad for the food and the warmth.

She rode for the rest of the morning without incident. The sun had just passed noon when she came to a fork in the way. Fleet chose the right hand. She had no sure plan in mind, and one way was the same as the other to her mind. At the worst, she might find a comfortable inn, have a good sleep, then be forced to retrace her steps and take the other fork on the morrow.

At least she hoped that might be the worst.

The road widened as she traveled until it became a large, well-tended thoroughfare. It was paved with smooth stone and lined by large, shapely trees that now bore the last of fall's vivid colors. Rain dripped off the leaves, misted down to soak her hair, rolled down Fleet's forelock and finally dripped off his nose.

Large, wrought-iron gates appeared suddenly out of the mist before her. She passed under them, unchecked. Smooth bluish-gray stone stretched out before her, wet and slick, unmarred by either muddy footstep or hoofprint. No merchant's wagon rolled along, no knight cantered by on his proud steed, no freeman walked off to the side with his gear on his back and his liberty leaving him with his head held high. It was as if the entire world slept.

Was this the magic people spoke of when they talked about the vale of sorcery that protected the palace of Neroche? She had thought there might have been paths that dead-ended, terrible monsters that faded in and out of the mist, ghostly shapes that led travelers into deep bogs and trapped them there. This mere bit of emptiness was, in her opinion, not very substantial and certainly nothing to inspire legend and nervous whispers.

She hadn't gone but a mile farther when the road turned into a formal approach. She lifted her eyes and saw what she could only assume was the king's palace, standing in the distance. A heavy mist hung over the parapets, obscuring the towers. Darkness crept down the walls and pooled at the footing of the bulwarks.

Mehar shivered.

She rode slowly up to the entrance. Magic lay draped over the massive palace like a loosely woven piece of very soft cloth that fell onto and covered every stone, sank into every crenellation, cascaded down onto every flat surface. Mehar slid down off Fleet's back and walked up the dozen very wide steps that led to the front door. She reached out and smoothed her hand over the illusion, finding it as soft as cottonwood fluff but strong, as if it had been forged by a steel smith at the height of his powers.

Mehar looked back at Fleet and decided she would leave him where he was. There was grass where he stood and he would be safe enough there for a time.

She turned back to the palace and studied the illusion that covered it. Suddenly, she saw where it might be parted, as if it were two curtains that had been drawn together. She lifted one side of the spell, then came to an abrupt halt, staring in horror at the ruin the spell had concealed.

The king's crest that had no doubt once hung proudly over the massive front doors now lay shattered on the steps. She picked her way over the shards of fine plaster and eased past doors that hung drunkenly from twisted hinges.

Where was the king?

Where was his mage?

She found, to her shame, that it troubled her far more that the mage might be lost than the king. She supposed there were a handful of princes or perhaps a cousin or two in line for the throne, but what would they do without a mage to guide them?

She picked her way through the ruined corridors, stumbling a time or two quite heavily over large bits of tumbled marble she hadn't seen in the gloom. Her hands bore the brunt of those falls, but her knees wound up bloody in time as well. But she found that she couldn't turn back, so she pressed on until she reached what had obviously been the palace's great hall.

She stepped inside the doorway, then froze.

Stones from the hall floor had been tossed up and about without care for where they landed. Furniture had been reduced to firewood. Tapestries were shredded, plates and bowls scattered like seeds on the wind, walls were pockmarked. She walked into the hall in a daze, tripped over a stone, and sat down heavily on a bit of something that crunched beneath her. She remained where she was for some time and simply marveled at the extent of the destruction.

And then she realized with a start that she was not alone. A man had come into the hall from an entrance across from her. Who was he? A palace servant? A common peasant? A trespasser? She watched his shadowy figure as he kindled a fire in a hollow of the floor that had once been a no-doubt quite lovely bit of polished stone. He seemed perfectly comfortable in his surroundings, which gave her pause. Did he know that everyone in the palace was dead?

Had he been the one to do the deed?

"Cousin, damn you, where are you—"

The voice came closer, accompanied by sounds of various bits of flesh encountering various other bits of unyielding palace—and that accompanied by a litany of very inventive curses—until the voice and its creator stumbled into the great hall with a final *damnation.*

Mehar recognized the man instantly. He could possibly add an empty belly to the list of things that had bothered him during the past few hours.

"What the devil have you been doing?" the man demanded. "I've been scouting, I was *assaulted* by a band of ruffians who stole my breakfast, and here you sit as if you have nothing better to do than sulk!"

"I am not sulking," the other man said, sitting down with a sigh. "I am thinking."

"Well, you should think less and *do* more," the other man said in a disgruntled voice as he stomped into and across the chamber. He righted a bench only to realize that it was missing a leg. He tossed it aside with another curse, then sat on a wobbly stone that looked as if it had erupted from the floor. "What a bloody mess!" he exclaimed, holding his hands against the fire. "Why don't you *do* something—"

Mehar looked over her shoulder and contemplated the distance to the doorway. It would only take one good leap to gain it, then she could flee and count the cost in bruises and blood later. What had she been thinking to come in here alone? For all she knew, these two had murdered her king and would next turn their blades on her. She crawled to her feet slowly and eased her way toward the yawning opening—

"Where's the light?" a voice said sharply. "How's a body to bring in a meal without a proper light?"

Mehar jumped out of the way as a brisk, gray-haired woman of indeterminate age marched through the doorway and over to the fire carrying a tray laden with things that made Mehar's mouth water. Despite her meal that morning, she still had days to make up for and what was over there looked fit for the king's finest table.

Maybe she'd said as much aloud without realizing it because quite suddenly the woman as well as the men turned and looked at her with varying degrees of surprise.

The man with a thousand curses dredged up a few more. "Thief," he said, pointing an accusing finger at her. "She stole my breakfast!"

"It looks as if she could have used it, Alcuin," the older woman said curtly. She handed him the tray, then marched across the chamber purposefully and pulled Mehar back along behind her toward the fire. "Come, gel, and eat."

"Nay, cast her from the hall," said the man named Alcuin. "Better yet, toss her in the dungeon. Nay, even better yet, put her to work. There's aught to be shoveled out of the stalls."

Mehar had certainly done enough of that over the course of her life—a daughter of Angesand took her turn like everyone else in caring for the family business—so she wasn't completely opposed to the idea, but she was opposed to losing her life and she couldn't say with any degree of confidence that she trusted any of the chamber's occupants.

"Mucking out the stalls?" the old woman echoed doubtfully. "Nay, what the gel needs is a rest. Alcuin, up and give her your seat."

"Won't," said Alcuin stubbornly.

The other man rose silently. "Take mine, lady."

Mehar opened her mouth to thank him, then caught a full view of him by the weak light of the fire. And whatever else she might have said, along with her few remaining wits, slipped through her grasp like fine silk.

It wasn't that he wasn't beautiful, for he was. It wasn't that he wasn't well-made and tall, for he was that as well. It was his eyes, crystal blue eyes full of shards of deeper blue and veins of white, eyes that laid her soul bare.

Fey. Fey and otherworldly. She didn't doubt that if this man had possessed any imagery at all, he could have been the one to wreak the havoc she stood in. Any thoughts of gratitude she had fled, to be replaced by ones of dread. She tried to speak. She croaked instead, something quite unintelligible.

He frowned at her. "Are you unwell?"

She gestured weakly around her. "Did you do this?"

"I should be flattered you think so, but nay, I did not."

"And why in the world would he—" Alcuin interrupted, but he was cut off by a sharp movement of the other's hand.

"What do you seek here, lady?" asked the man with the fathomless eyes.

Her answer came tumbling out before she could stop it. "I came to see the king. Well," she amended, "not the king really. One of his mages. The best mage, if possible, for I've questions for him. I suppose I could do with one less skilled, if I had to." She paused for a moment or two. "I don't suppose any of his mages still live," she said slowly.

"Unfortunately, they don't," the man said.

"And the king?"

"Dead as well."

Hope extinguished itself in her breast. Now the illusion hanging over the castle made sense. It was obviously just the remnants of a former magic.

"What of his son, the prince?"

"He was with the king," came the answer.

"Of course," she said. "And what of the others—"

"Enough of this," said the old woman. She took Mehar by the arm and pulled her away from the fire. "What you need, gel, is a seat by a proper cooking fire with as much to eat as you like and I, Cook, will see as you gets it. Did you come on a horse? Does it need tending?"

"She did," Alcuin said. "It's trimming the flowerbeds near the hall door."

"Then one of you lads can go see to him," Cook said. "For now, my gel, you should eat. Everything will seem better with something in your belly."

Mehar couldn't answer. Not only did Cook not offer her the opportunity, she doubted she could have found words if she'd needed them.

The king was dead.

Worse still, his mage was dead.

And if that wasn't enough, her father had a price on her head.

She doubted those were things Cook's stew could change.

She paused at the archway that led to the kitchens and looked back over her shoulder. The two peasants were still there, the taller one still standing where she'd left him, staring at her with those odd eyes of his. She shivered, her former doubts about him returning. He looked infinitely capable of a great number of sinister things. She supposed if she'd had any sense at all, she would have fled as fast as her feet would carry her.

But apparently her common sense had been left behind with her cloak. She was cold, hungry, and exhausted. Perhaps if she remained in the kitchen, she would avoid any of that man's untoward magic—for she was almost positive he had some.

The thought that she might possibly ask him for aid flitted across her mind, but she let it disappear on its way just as quickly. She turned away from that perilous stranger and followed Cook to the promise of peace and safety—or at least a decent meal, which would give her the strength to find peace and safety.

It would have to do.

Chapter Two

In Which Gilraehen the Prince Finds Himself Pretending to be Someone He's Not...

The lights twinkled in the deep blue vault of the palace ballroom. The dancers, garbed in luxurious silks of rainbow hues, swirled about the marbled floor; the sweet strains of song played on rare instruments by the realm's finest players wove themselves through the air, in and out of the dancers' patterns. Lights floated on the air, occasionally fluttering down to land on the delighted faces of the occupants of the chamber. The lady of the hall looked over the guests; it was she who made the lights dance with the slightest movement of her fingers. The lord looked on as well, watching his guests with a benevolent smile, pleased at their pleasure.

"Dam*nation*!"

And so the spell was broken. Gil blinked and looked at his cousin, who had tripped over something and gone sprawling. He sighed. The only things dancing now were tumbled bits of marble; the only things floating presently through the air were dust mores up by the passage of his cursing cousin. His mother, the queen, was dead. His father, the king, was dead as well. His brothers had vanished on the field of battle and his father's palace was in ruins. If he'd had a sense of humor, he would have said he'd had better days. But he didn't have a sense of humor. In fact, he wondered if he would ever again smile at anything, much less laugh. Any merriment he'd possessed had been lost somewhere on that horrendous journey back from Pevenry, from whence he'd fled like a kicked whelp—

Someone must be left alive, Gilraehen, his father had gasped as his life ebbed from him. *Flee, hide, gather your strength to fight another day.*

Gil hadn't wanted to flee, nor hide, nor take the time to gather his strength. He'd wanted to turn, to ride onto the field, and find his enemy to run him through. Never mind that his enemy was his great-great-uncle. Never mind that the power Lothar wielded was immense, or that he had twisted the same to his own ends until it had become something unrecognizable and evil. Never mind that Gil had exhausted almost all the reserves of his own power trying to protect his father's army. Lothar deserved death and Gil had been more than willing to aid him in finding it and finishing the war his sire, Alexandir, had begun with that vast, well-trained army.

The army that had almost completely perished.

And why was it that he, Gilraehen the Fey, prince of the house of Neroche, had survived whilst all around him were lost? It was because he'd taken the bloodied hilt of the sword his father had managed to lift up toward him and bolted, leaving those about him to die in agony of soul and body both. Last night, he'd led that woman to believe that the prince had died on the field with his father. In a certain sense, he wasn't sure that wasn't true—

A sharp slap brought him to himself without delay. Alcuin, his cousin and part of the reason he himself was still alive, damn him, stood with his hand pulled back, apparently prepared to deliver another bracing blow.

Gil glared at him. "You dare much."

Alcuin grunted, unimpressed. "Brooding on the past serves nothing. Put it behind you."

Aye, put it behind him like the smoking field he'd put behind him. With one last, vast sweep of his matchless power, he'd set the whole bloody place afire. For anyone to have survived that—be he man, beast, or monster—would have been a miracle. Unfortunately, he knew there would be at least one to survive, the one man alive with power greater than his, who would no doubt come seeking him in his own good time.

"In truth, I don't much care to remember that escape," Alcuin muttered. "Don't know why you do."

Because it was constantly before him, the sight of that endlessly thick wall of Lothar's misshapen men, the smell of their sweat, the feel of his boots sloshing through their blood that soaked the ground, the heat of the fire behind him, driving him forward without choice. He and Alcuin had started with twenty men of their household, but by the end of his flight, it had been naught but him and Alcuin on their own legs, with only Alcuin's stubbornness to keep them alive.

Alcuin clapped a hand on his shoulder and shook him. "Gil, stop," he said. "Stop thinking so damned much."

"What else do you suggest I do?" Gil demanded, irritated. "Go on holiday to the seaside and leave my realm in shreds?"

"You have no realm," Alcuin said pleasantly. "You haven't even found your father's crown—not that anyone with any authority is about to put it on your head should you find it, though I suppose I would do in a pinch—and you have no army. You don't even have anywhere to sleep, unless you've been scooping up feathers and stuffing them back into your mattress whilst I was out taking my life in my hands and scouring the countryside for ne'er-do-wells."

"And finding yourself and your breakfast bested by a girl half your size," Gil noted. "Some scout, you."

"She caught me unawares. Now," Alcuin continued, "since you insist on squandering all that magic you have at your disposal in a misguided effort to appear as a common man—a useless exercise, if you ask me, for even I can sense what you are—then you must rely on the paltry skills of those sworn to serve you to keep the kingdom safe. At least my scouting, such as it was, yielded nothing but an empty belly. None of Lothar's minions—unless you want to count the wench. What do you think of her, by the by?" he added with a look of unwilling interest. "She could do with a tidy-up, I daresay, though I suppose Lothar's spies have looked worse —"

"She isn't one of his spies," Gil said. He had no idea who she was, nor why she was riding a beast such as the one he'd put away in the stable the evening before, but she had no taint of evil on her. He took a deep breath that was suddenly full of her, full of the smell of herbs and flowers, and the sweet scent of sunshine.

He pulled his mind abruptly away from that image. He rubbed his gritty eyes and cast about for something else to think on.

Her horse, aye, that was it. Now, there was a beast to dream about; never had he seen its equal. Last night he'd wondered if he would get it to cover without it tearing him to shreds. He'd managed it only because he'd finally convinced the beast — in less than dulcet tones — that his bloody mistress was filling her belly at a fine fire and would be along afterwards to see to him.

Whether she had done the like he didn't know because he'd put the horse up, then spent half the night walking through his ruined gardens. He'd finally cast himself upon his previously quite plump goose-feather mattress and partaken of two full hours of sleep before nightmares had driven him out of dreaming, and he'd come back to the great, formerly grand hall to brood.

"Isn't this the first place he'll look for us?" Alcuin asked suddenly. "You know," he said, his voice lowering, "*him.*"

"Aye, I knew of whom you spoke," Gil said wearily. "And what I'm hoping for is that he'll think I died on the field. He'll realize soon enough that I didn't, but by then I will have a plan."

"If you say so," Alcuin said, sounding quite doubtful that Gil might manage something that complicated. "And I suppose I'll follow you, just as I have since we were five and both had our arses blistered because of *your* damned idiotic idea to try a few spells from one of your mother's locked books. How did you open the lock on that large, black, obviously unsuitable-for-wee-lads book of sorcery anyway?"

The memory of that was almost enough to lighten Gil's heart. "I touched it and it fell open."

Alcuin stared at him in silence. Well, not complete silence. There was the incessant *drip, drip, drip* of something leaking onto the unyielding marble floor. Gil wondered what the floor would look like when the rains of fall truly began.

"Then, perhaps," Alcuin said finally, "someday you will touch Lothar's defenses and they will fall open in like manner. It could happen." He smiled grimly. "I could also march into the kitchen and find myself something delicious to eat that hadn't come from things that we've been storing for just such a disaster as this. Cook is a wonder, but even she can't make sprouted grain any less unappetizing than it is." He turned and started toward the far door, the one that led to the kitchens. "Perhaps unappetizing is the wrong word. It would just be a damned sight more interesting if I just had a bit of fancy marmalade to go with it. Currant jam, perhaps. A smidgen of honey..."

Gil left the hall by a different door. He had no stomach for either currant jam or honey, even if any could be found. He picked his way around the heaps of rubble strewn all about the formerly quite impressive passageway that led from the front doors to many of the king's other receiving chambers, and wished for a large broom.

He left the palace, ignoring the ruin of his father's crest on the front steps, and continued on to the stables. There, at least, something had been left standing. It was puzzling, the extent of the destruction. No one could have wreaked this kind of havoc without either a vast army or a goodly amount of magery at his disposal. Lothar's army had been on the field. Perhaps one of Lothar's sons had come calling whilst he was away.

It was almost more than he could bear to think on.

He entered the stables, stopped, and breathed deeply. Ah, to have nothing more pressing demanding his attention than a few horses needing to be groomed. He'd certainly passed much of his youth doing just that. At the moment, he would have given much to work in the stables and ignore the burdens of his birthright.

Though the claiming of that duty was still before him, as Alcuin had so pointedly reminded him. He did have his father's crown (hidden cunningly under what was left of his bed) but he had no one to install that fine bit of jewel-encrusted metal atop his head, unless he was to send for his mother's father, a feisty old man of impeccable lineage and questionable wisdom in matters of his personal safety; or his uncle, his mother's brother, who had sequestered himself on an island half a kingdom away where he might think deep thoughts in peace. Neither man would come willingly, but perhaps they could be persuaded. Later, when Gil had found a kingdom to rule. For now, he had more pressing matters to attend to.

Mainly that of watching the woman sitting beneath the poor light coming in from a stable window, poring over a book.

He stood in the shadows and stared at her, wondering who she was and how it was she had come to the palace by herself. He knew few women who traveled alone in such perilous times; it must have been something overwhelmingly compelling to have driven her from her home without aid.

Especially given the look of her.

He scrutinized her whilst he had the chance. To be sure, she had not the painful type of beauty of those who regularly came to court—generally at their fathers' insistence—to present themselves to him and curry his favor. He had, in his long, weary existence as the heir to the throne, seen more beautiful women than he cared to number. But never had he met a woman who troubled his dreams after a mere glance into her eyes.

He jumped slightly when he realized she was looking at him. He bowed. "My pardon, lady. I came to make sure you were well."

She shut her book and stood, looking as if she might just flee. "My thanks, good sir," she said quickly. "I've had a fine meal or two, so I'll soon be on my way."

Nay was almost out of his mouth before he grasped at the few remaining shreds of good sense he normally possessed and stopped himself. Nay, he was loath to let her leave, but there was no good reason to force her to stay.

At least none that he could come up with at present.

All the same, there was no sense in her rushing off hastily. Better that she continue on her quest fully fed and much better rested. It was only common courtesy that demanded that he offer her the chance for both. His mother would have been greatly impressed by his comportment.

And appalled by his subterfuge.

The woman shifted, as if she intended to bolt for the door.

"Sit," he commanded, and she flinched. He took a deep breath. "Please sit," he amended, "and take your ease. No need to rush off."

She sat slowly, but didn't look away, as if she expected him to leap upon her at any moment and throttle her.

He smiled, trying to project an air of harmlessness. It wasn't something he did well, but he tried. He cast about for something to distract her. "Your book," he said, nodding at it. "It looks well worn."

She ran her hand carefully over the leather cover. "It was my mother's."

"Is it a tale about her life?"

She studied him for a moment before she answered slowly. "Nay, 'tis a book of spells."

He blinked. Books of spells were rare and guarded jealously. "Are they interesting spells?"

"I don't know. I can't read them."

"Then 'tis for that reason you sought the king's mage?"

"Aye, but now I find that my journey was in vain."

He hesitated. To reveal his skill with magery was to reveal his own identity and he found himself with a sudden desire to be, for a day or two, simply Gil and not the fey Prince of Neroche. It wouldn't hurt to let this woman believe him to be less than he was and allow his skill with spells to lie fallow, would it? He found the plan to his liking and proceeded with its implementation without hesitation. Ordinary, unremarkable conversation was to be the order of the day.

"Well," he said, "at least your journey was made on a fine horse."

"Aye," she agreed.

He waited, but she offered nothing else. "Is he yours?" he asked.

"He is now."

His eyebrows went up of their own accord. "Did you steal him?"

She smiled briefly and the sight of her faint smile did something to his heart, something he feared he might not recover from anytime soon.

"Steal him?" she asked, then shook her head. "I wouldn't call it that. I needed to flee an unsavory betrothal and Fleet was the fastest way to do it."

An unsavory betrothal? That was nothing unusual, but fleeing on such a steed certainly was. "And how will your sire feel about that?" Gil asked.

"I've no doubt it inspired him to put a price on my head for the deed."

He was surprised she seemed so at ease with that. "Who is this sire who is so ruthless?"

She shifted on her seat. "No one of importance."

"I'm curious."

"I fear you'll need to remain so."

He smiled to himself; her lack of deference was quite refreshing. "Then I don't suppose you'll give me your bridegroom's name, either, will you?"

"I don't suppose I will."

"Was he young or old?"

She smiled briefly, without humor. "Old enough to be my sire, and quite cruel."

He pursed his lips. Somehow the thought was one that seemed particularly loathsome in regard to the woman before him. She deserved sunshine, youth, long days spent searching for flowers for her table, not a cold existence in some dotard's mean hall devoid of even the smallest comforts.

The mystery of her was becoming unsettlingly compelling. "What is your name, lady?" he asked. "Might I have that at least?"

"And what would you do with that name, if you had it?"

"Use it," he said simply.

She looked into the distance for so long, he began to wonder if she had forgotten his question. Then she sighed suddenly and looked at him. "I am trusting you with more than just my name if I give it to you."

He nodded seriously. "Aye."

She put her shoulders back and took a deep breath. "Mehar. My name is Mehar."

"Mehar," he repeated. "A beautiful name. An unusual name." One he desperately wished he recognized, but there were, he could personally attest, a staggering number of unwed maidens in his kingdom, so not being able to fix a place to a name wasn't unthinkable. Perhaps it would come to him in time.

"And what of your name?" she prompted. "Cook called you Gil—"

"...bert," he replied promptly. "Gilbert. Or Gilford, if you like better. My father never could decide. Gilford was his favorite hound and Gilbert was a mighty rooster that pleased him and so he had a goodly amount of trouble selecting what he thought would suit..." He trailed off with a shrug, wondering if he were lying well.

She only stared at him suspiciously.

Apparently he wasn't a good liar. "Call me Gil," he finished.

"Gil," she repeated. "Is that your name?"

"It will do until you trust me enough to tell me who your sire is."

She smiled and seemed to thaw just a bit. "Very well. For now, Gil, who may or may not be named after a mighty fowl, favor me with an answer or two. Why do you find yourself in this ruined place?"

"I was born here," he admitted.

"Did you serve the king?"

"Aye, that as well."

"What happened to his kingdom?"

"He gathered his army and went to battle Lothar of Wych-weald."

"In truth?" she asked, surprised. "I thought the black mage of Wychweald was long dead by now."

"Oh, nay, he is very much alive," Gil said, pushing aside the vision of Lothar's' fathomless black eyes and the mocking smile he'd worn as he'd watched Gil pay the price for daring to battle him. "I daresay the king grew tired of losing his people to Lothar's service. Lothar does that, you know. Presses innocent souls into serving him. By the time he's finished with them, you wouldn't recognize them as human."

She shivered. "I daresay. Then did you go to battle as well?"

"Aye, with my father. But my father did not return."

"I'm sorry."

"Aye, I am as well."

She stared at him for a moment or two in silence, then she sighed and stood. "Thank you for your name, and the pleasant conversation, but I should now be about seeing to my charges, so I can earn my supper."

He watched her look for a place to put her book. "I could hold that," he offered. "I could also help you with the horses."

"Are you a stable's lad, then?"

"I have spent my share of time here," he said.

She hesitated, looked at him carefully a moment or two more, then handed him her book. "I'll see to the horses. You look a bit soft."

He spluttered before he realized she was teasing him.

"If you flee with my book, Fleet will hunt you down," she added. "You would regret it."

Gil didn't doubt it. He accepted the book with what he hoped was a look of trustworthiness and sat down with a manly grunt on the hay. He turned to the first page, fully prepared to find some obscure village witch's spells, scribbled in an illegible hand.

Instead, he found a hand that was learned. The characters were neat and precise, with a flowing script that pleased the eye. He read through several pages, his wonder growing with each until he finally stopped halfway through the book, closed the halves together slowly, and stared off into the stable's gloom thoughtfully.

The spells were of Camanaë. He was so surprised to find something of theirs in his hand, he hardly knew what to think. There were few of that particular school of magic left in the world.

They were, after all, one of Lothar's preferred targets.

He knew none of them personally. By reputation, he knew them to be mostly wizardesses. There was the occasional mage who'd been gifted his mother's power, of course, when occasion required, but for the most part they were women, keepers of a surprisingly strong magic. If the magic he had inherited from his sire was full of ruling, Camanaë's was full of healing, of protection, of restoring after the ruling hand had done its brutal work.

He looked at Mehar thoughtfully as she groomed her horse and wondered if the genealogy kept by the court mage would aid him in discovering the identity of her mother. Unfortunately, he feared that Tagaire of Neroche was dead, which meant that he himself would be the one doing the searching. He had a brief vision of Tagaire's terrifyingly unorganized chamber, with stacks of paper, pots, and sundry falling off tables and spilling out of shelves, and decided that he would leave the search alone.

For the moment.

He watched Mehar for a bit longer before he rose and took over her tasks. He groomed the rest of the horses, feeling her eyes on him, and finding his hands fumbling much more than they should have.

A very unsettling feeling, on the whole.

But an hour later, the tasks were done and he was walking with her back to the palace.

"I think I can aid you with a spell or two," he offered casually.

"You?"

He smiled at her disbelief. "Aye, me. I'm not completely ignorant of things magical." Though Camanaë was not his own magic, his schooling had demanded that he learn the languages of all the various sorts of magics out in the world. He could not only decipher Mehar's book, he could likely weave a spell or two from it.

A dreadful hope bloomed in her face. "Could you?"

"I could." That hope touched a place in his heart he'd been sure Lothar had incinerated along with his hand. He had to take a deep breath before he could speak again. "I could also see to your hand, the one you favor. A bad burn?"

"From Alcuin's rabbit."

"A high price to pay for something that probably took him all morning to catch."

"I paid him well for that hare."

Gil grunted. "Trust him not to say as much. Come, then, and let us find you somewhere more comfortable to stay than a mean scrap of floor in Cook's domain."

She walked with him along the ruined path, holding tightly to her book. "Where? In the roosting place of some fine noble perhaps?"

"Nothing less. When the king is out, the peasants shout."

She smiled. "Did you make that up yourself?"

"This very moment."

"Then you'd best hope none of the king's relations return, or they'll have your head for the shouting you've done in the hall."

"I've tried to tidy up the place as best I could."

"Hmmm," she said, sounding quite unconvinced. "Well, perhaps some of the king's people will come back and see to things."

"Aye," he said, but he found himself less distracted by the thought of his people returning to see to work he could manage with a slight bit of effort himself than he was by the sight of Mehar-of-someplace-she-wouldn't-name with her riotous hair and her serious gray eyes.

Which was so completely inappropriate considering who he was and what his future held that he could only shake his head at himself.

But that didn't stop him from inviting her and her book to come with him to supper where they might all become better acquainted.

Poor fool that he was.

Chapter Three

In Which Mehar Finds More Than Dust Under the Prince's Bed...

Mehar sat at the high table in the palace's grand hall and watched as a long-fingered hand followed the words written on a page, then traced a pattern on the wood of the table, showing her how the spell should be woven. It was a spell of protection.

Mehar didn't wonder that it was the first spell in her mother's book.

She did wonder, however, how it was that a mere peasant, his youth spent in the king's palace aside, should know how to weave such a spell with such unfaltering confidence. She looked up at him, met his searing blue eyes and felt herself being woven into a weft that seemed like threads of a destiny she'd never anticipated.

"Here," he said, nodding toward his hand, "watch again, then copy me."

He traced the pattern again, a simple pattern that seemed suddenly to make perfect sense to her. Mehar copied his motions, then stared in astonishment as silver lines appeared where she had traced, as if she'd written with ink that shimmered and glittered and was slow to fade.

She looked at Gil. He was staring at her in astonishment.

"Well," he said at length. "Apparently you have a gift. I daresay you have it from your mother."

"Why do you say that?"

"Because Camanaë is a matriarchal magic. If your dam had it, then so would you. Do you have sisters?"

She looked up at him. "Aye."

"Then they have it as well, unless they're completely dim-witted."

"I'll have to think on that," she said. "I tried a spell of un-noticing on them and it failed miserably. I thought it was because I'd woven it poorly, but perhaps they merely possessed the wherewithal to see through it." She smiled, chagrined. "I never credited them with any skill at all beyond the ability to attend to their potions and beautifiers for great stretches of time. Perhaps I misjudged them."

"Perhaps, or they might be totally lacking in any imagination at all," he conceded. "In which case it would take a great need to awaken whatever magic is in their blood. Have they any great needs?"

"None beyond accurate looking glasses," she said dryly. It was quite an extraordinary thought, though, to imagine that her sisters might have inherited something from their mother besides her perfect beauty.

It was also a marvel to find herself tracing lines on a table, beautiful lines that looked as if a wizard had done the like, yet they had come from her humble, work-roughened hand with its chipped fingernails and cracked skin.

"Well," she said, finding herself at quite a loss. Then she looked at Gil and found herself traveling even farther down that uncharted path to complete bewilderment.

How could she have known two weeks ago that a fortnight passed in fear would find her sitting in the palace at Neroche, at the high table no less, sketching bits of magic on that royal table and having it come to her hand as if it found her pleasing to its purposes?

"I think I like this," she said finally.

He smiled. "I imagine you do."

She gestured at the table. "My lines are better than yours."

He laughed. "Aye, and so they would be, for my magic is not of Camanaë, lady. And that is a good thing, else we would have no... else we would be—"

She watched him squirm as he found himself pinioned quite thoroughly by a lie he was obviously not equipped to spew forth.

"Magic? You have magic?" she asked politely. "What kind? Educate me, good sir."

He pursed his lips. "I inherited a few bits from my sire."

"A little prevarication, that," she noted.

"And a bit more from my dam."

She waited patiently.

"All right," he grumbled, "a great bit from both parents, but I'll not tell you more until you tell me why a woman of your beauty travels alone to a king's palace on a horse Angesand himself would salivate over, with a book of magic that dark mages far and wide would kill her for, and she hides her name as if revealing it to a soul as trustworthy as myself might endanger her to just those sorts of villains." He looked at her crossly. "You tell me that first."

Beauty. Had he said beauty? Mehar found herself with an alarming redness creeping with unnerving speed up her throat and onto her cheeks.

Gil nodded in satisfaction. "I agree. 'Tis quite embarrassing when one realizes that one is being unnecessarily stubborn."

"I told you there was a price on my head," Mehar said evenly, her blush receding at the thought, "and how do I know you wouldn't find it a sum worthy of your attention? It isn't as if you're dressing yourself in embroidered silks and reclining upon cushions of uncommon softness with covers woven of cashmere."

He looked at the table and traced her pattern with his own. The lines faded after his passing, but they didn't disappear. Instead, they glowed a deep blue, shot with silver.

That was an uncommon magic, his.

But then he brushed his hand over the wood and the lines disappeared. He looked at her.

"There is no sum that I would consider to be worth your head."

"Are you so rich?" she asked.

"Nay, I am so honorable."

She pressed her hand flat on the table, over the place where they'd both woven her mother's spell, but found no adequate reply to his words.

"And if you would learn them from me," he continued, "I can teach you a spell or two of ward, another of strengthening whatever weapon you have to hand, and perhaps one or two that might aid you when someone is set to come upon you."

"Where did you learn all this?" she asked. "You, a simple peasant."

He smiled at her and a dimple appeared in his cheek, a mark of such easy charm that she found herself quite enchanted. It was with an effort that she looked away from it.

"Haimert of Wexham, the court mage, wasn't always about the king's business," he said. "When he had a free moment, I bribed him for knowledge with Cook's most easy-to-carry pasties. It seemed to us both a fair trade."

"Do you have great power?"

He opened his mouth to speak, then shut it, and smiled at her. "Enough for my purposes, and telling more would tell you all—" He stopped and looked up as Alcuin came into the hall and walked quickly over to the table. "Aye?" he asked.

Mehar watched Alcuin's gaze flick to her and back to Gil. Gil turned to smile at her.

"Perhaps you would care for a bit of peace," he offered, "in that luxurious chamber I promised you."

She was tempted to tell them she would rather stay and listen, but she forbore. "I'll leave you lads to your plotting," she said as she rose, "though what two peasants would have to plot about I can't imagine, unless you're bent on making off with the king's finest silver in which case I should likely put a stop to it. Are you planning thievery?"

Alcuin snorted. "Nay, we are not."

Well, it was obvious they had business together, and as she just couldn't believe anything foul of Gil truly, her first impressions aside, she left the grand hall with an untroubled heart. Soon deep whispers were sliding along the walls to either side of her and rising up to flutter against the ceiling, whispers that carried the hint of subterfuge.

There was more to those peasants than met the eye.

She threaded her way through the ruble in the corridor, wandering down passageway after passageway, becoming hopelessly lost, but she suspected that had less to do with Gil's directions than it did with her own distracted state.

She had woven a spell from her mother's book and had it fall easily from her hand.

She felt as if she had just put her foot to a path that had been laid out before her all along; she just hadn't been able to see it. It was, on the whole, a vastly unsettling feeling, but even that had an air of familiarity that sent chills down her spine.

She paused before the door she thought might be the correct one, then eased it open and peeked inside. The chamber was empty. She entered it, then slowly shut the heavy door behind her. The ruin here was not so terrible as it was in other places. The tapestries, for the most part, were still intact. The furniture was merely overturned, not destroyed. She pushed away from the door and wandered about the chamber, putting things to rights. She sat on the bed and wondered just whose chamber she was in. The king's, perhaps?

But nay, there were no kingly trappings, no gilding, no banners with his crest, no furs and luxurious silks hanging on the walls. But the colors on the rugs, the hangings, and the bedclothes had been dyed with difficulty and at no doubt great expense.

There was a bench sitting under the window, and next to that a chair sporting quite worn cushions, as if it had seen much use by one who sat and stared out the window to contemplate deep thoughts. She stared at the chair for a moment, then realized what struck her as odd. There was a blanket draped over its arm, as if it had been just recently used and not quite put away properly. It was a cloth she recognized.

She likely should, given that she'd been the one to weave it.

She floated over to the chair, feeling as if her legs were no longer beneath her. She lifted the cloth and held it to her cheek, remembering vividly the weaving of it.

It had been for the eldest of Alexandir the Bold's sons, a gift sent to comfort him after his mother had been slain. Fey, that eldest prince had been rumored to be, fey and wild. People tended to make all manner of signs to ward off any stray spells or whatnot when they spoke of him. Mehar had imagined that he was less strange than sorrowful, and it was for that reason that she'd woven her gift for him.

She sank down into the chair, set her book onto the nearby bench, and pulled the prince's blanket over herself. She had one of her own, something her mother had woven for her the month before she'd died, but hers had been destroyed along with everything else. She fingered the cloth. It was frayed in placed, faded by the sun in others, missing bits of the fringe she had painstakingly tied. She leaned her head back against the chair, closed her eyes, and spared a brief thought for the prince who had obviously used this often.

Had he died alongside his father, or had he been alone? Was he in a better place? She'd often wondered where a man went when his task here was finished. Her mother had told her, with her eyes full of its vision, that she saw a land far beyond the eastern deserts, where the air was cool and the waters clear, and there was no more suffering.

She hoped, as she rubbed the prince's soft blanket against her cheek, that he had found such a place. Perhaps he now sat at table with his mother who had gone before him. She closed her eyes and wept, not daring to hope that such a place existed, or that she might one day feel her own mother's arms around her yet again, smell the sweet scent of her, feel the gentle caress of her hand on her own hair.

She wept until the wool was damp and began to disturb her. She sat up, folded the blanket over the arm of the chair, then winced at the brightness of the setting sun streaming through the window. She turned away from the window and watched the motes of dust dance. They glinted and sparkled as they swirled and slid toward the floor.

Then other things began to glint.

She blinked at the sight of something sparkling beneath the bed.

She rose from the chair, then dropped to her hands and knees and peered more closely under the wooden railing. She reached in and drew out something quite unexpected.

A crown.

She put her hand under again and drew out, with quite a bit more difficulty, a sword.

She stared down at the treasures before her and wondered why they found themselves under this bed instead of upon the king's head and by his side where they should have been. Had the king left them behind? The crown, she could understand. It had to get in one's way, when one was trying to avoid having his head cut off in battle. Though with the gems that encrusted that substantial circle of metal, she was surprised the king hadn't worn it in hopes that the glint of gemmery would have blinded his enemies and won him the day by its virtue alone.

The sword was a deeper puzzle. That the king should have left that behind was unthinkable. Gil had said he was a servant of the king, so perhaps he had brought his liege's sword back from the field of battle for him, that he might give it to one who might in future times come to claim the kingship.

Odd, though, that they should find themselves here.

She returned both the sword and the crown to their places, then turned her mind from the king's gear to things that concerned her more closely.

She had found someone who could help her understand her

mother's book. She had a warm place to sleep and decent food in return for work she could readily do. It was enough, at least, for the moment.

She rose, fetched the prince of Neroche's blanket, then cast herself upon the bed and fell asleep, its softness surrounding her with a quiet peace.

Chapter Four

*In Which Gilraehen Finds Himself Fixed Quite
Firmly on the Horns of a Dilemma...*

G il had never considered himself a poor horseman, but he found himself quite out of his depth at present. He watched Mehar fly, and he meant that quite literally, over a hedge that any sensible gardener would have trimmed whilst standing upon a ladder. He himself chose quite wisely to direct his own mount around the greenery instead of over it. Mehar's horse, that fleet beast, was truly a miracle, and his rider was his equal in every respect. Robert of Angesand would have been proud to call her his.

Gil hauled back on his reins, then blinked in the manner he normally reserved for the break of day when it came too early.

Was Fleet one of Angesand's beasts?

It was possible.

Was Mehar one of Angesand's daughters?

That was possible as well.

He cast back to the times he'd been to Angesand's hall, but could only bring to mind three daughters; three beauties who were perfectly coiffed, perfectly mannered, and perfectly clean at all times. Not at all like the woman before him who had turned Fleet around and come cantering back his way.

She pulled up and laughed at him. "I thought you were for a goodly bit of speed this morn," she chided, "especially after the past three days you've spent just ambling through the gardens, yet here I find you merely sitting and admiring the divots in the grass."

Nay, I was admiring you was almost off his tongue before he thought better of it. Aye, admiring her with her hair tumbling down over her shoulders, her clothes splattered with mud, the cloak he'd loaned her also splattered with mud. Aye, and there went her cheek, just as muddy, thanks to the back of her hand brushing away a stray bit of hair.

What he really needed was Tagaire alive and well and pouring over pages of the realm's genealogy so he might answer Gil's question for him. Gil ran through a list of evil dotards as potential suitors for Mehar—the same list he'd been contemplating during those three days spent ambling through the garden with her—but no one came immediately to mind save Uirsig of Hagoth. Hagoth was hardly out of mourning for his fourth wife, so there was little chance he was looking for another. Perhaps Mehar's undesirable betrothed was an elderly farmer with grown children who had looked to her for a bit of pleasure after his own wife's death.

The thought, unsurprisingly, left Gil with a rather strong desire to grind his teeth.

"Come on," she said, turning Fleet back toward the garden. "Keep up, if you can. And given your showing this morning, I very much doubt you'll manage it."

He couldn't remember the last time a woman had spoken to him with such an appalling lack of respect. He laughed just the same and tried to keep up.

And, as she had predicted he would, he failed.

But as he struggled to follow her over shrubbery, around fallen benches, and over large pits of his father's garden, he came more surely to the conclusion that Fleet was no simple horse breeder's finest and Mehar was no simple horse breeder's daughter. He watched in awe as she sent Fleet over another jump that no sensible woman would have attempted and no horse with any fear at all would have dared.

He finally managed to draw alongside her. "You are magnificent," he said simply.

"'Tis the horse," she said, with a breathless laugh. "He is unmatched."

"As are you. No wonder Angesand was loath to let either of you go."

The blood drained from her face. With a cry of dismay, she wheeled Fleet around and galloped off before he could gather his wits to call an apology after her. He congratulated himself on being right, but that glowing feeling was somewhat lost in the effort it took to chase her. He wouldn't have caught her at all if she hadn't ridden straight for the front door and been stopped by the large contingent of souls loitering there.

Damnation. He wasn't even going to have a chance to apologize before all hell broke loose. Gil sighed heavily. His future had arrived—and far too soon for his taste.

He reined his horse in and squared his shoulders against the frowns of disapproval he was receiving from an older man and a younger woman who sat at the head of the company that blocked the door. He moved next to Mehar. "Allow me to introduce you," he said, inclining his head toward his guests. "His Majesty, King Douglass of Penrhyn and his daughter, the Princess Tiare of Penrhyn."

Mehar looked at him in surprise. "How would you know?" she asked.

"He would know, you grubby little upstart, because I am his betrothed," Tiare said coldly. "Though at the moment I am having grave doubts about the advisability of wedding with..."—at this point words seemed to quite fail her as she raked Gil with a gaze that missed no splatter of mud, no matter how slight—"with... with a prince who masquerades as a common laborer. It all seems quite inadvisable."

"Prince?" Mehar echoed faintly. "Prince?"

"No longer the prince," Douglass said, chewing on his pipe, then removing it and sending Gil a rather steely glance. "He is the king. The mind reels at such a thought, but is it possible, Gilraehen, that the tales are true and your father is dead? Leaving you in charge?"

Gil had wondered, on previous occasions, if he might have misjudged Douglass, having thought his meanness to be due to a man of his small stature being allotted such a small portion in life. But now, he concluded that Douglass was unfortunately entirely unpalatable on his own merits alone.

How was it, Gil asked himself, that he found himself connected to the pair before him? Penrhyn was an insignificant little country, and it exported nothing save the sour wine that some found a delicacy. Its kings were forever looking for ways to improve their situations, which usually entailed wedding their daughters to those who might pour money into monarchial coffers so the kings might import the things they desired instead of grousing about the fact that they couldn't produce the like themselves.

That had been one reason for Douglass's enthusiasm over Gil's betrothal to the quite tart Tiare.

Penrhyn also held, in a handful of quite inconsequential mountains, several mines of brencara, the sapphire gem that was quite necessary to the weaving of the spell of secrecy that covered the vale of Neroche. Gil's father had counseled him that it would be advisable to cement a supply of that rare gem far into the future. Gil was quite certain that the necessary spells could be cast with naught but his own two hands to aid him—indeed, he had proved that to himself the first time his father had suggested a match with the violently acerbic woman before him. He supposed his father had, in his heart of hearts, been less taken by the fact that Tiare had also been one of the few who hadn't begged to wed Gil because of his fierce beauty (their words and not his), and the delicious peril of putting themselves in his questionable hands, than he had been taken by the thought of a steady stream of sour wine running into his kingly cup.

Either that, or his father had suffered a complete and utter loss of good sense and betrothed his eldest son to Dour Douglass's nastiest daughter after one too many glasses of that sour wine.

Gil couldn't have said.

All he knew was that he was committed to a course he was quite sure he no longer wanted to pursue, without an out in sight.

Damn it anyway.

He swung down off his horse with a sigh and nodded to his guests. "If I might offer you the hospitality of my hall?" he asked politely.

Tiare rolled her eyes, her father made a sour face and a noise to match, then they both clambered down off horses that had seen far too much wear. And whilst they were about their journeys to the ground, Gil murmured a spell under his breath. The strength of it took a good deal of his own, and it certainly hadn't been a proper job—there was a good deal of screeching coming from inside the corridor in which his name figured prominently in uncomplimentary ways—but at least most of the castle was again put to rights.

He hoped that hadn't been a mistake. If evil eyes had been watching, there had certainly been magic there to be seen.

"Here, wench, come take our horses," Douglass said, gesturing behind Gil.

Gil opened his mouth to speak, but given that his breath had been taken away by what he'd just done, he didn't manage it. He leaned against his horse for a moment or two, then found himself eased aside as Mehar took the reins from him. She looked at him briefly with all the expression wiped off her face.

"With your leave, my liege?" she asked.

He would have scowled at her, or at least reminded her that she hadn't been all that forthcoming with her details, though he supposed he should have been quick enough to know that the only horse breeder who could generate the kind of stallion Fleet was would indeed be Robert of Angesand. But he didn't, mostly because he didn't have the breath for it.

"Gilraehen, go bathe," Tiare said crisply. "You look no better than that filthy peasant there."

He looked at Tiare quietly, quite steadily, and with no lack of warning—or so he intended it. Tiare returned his look, quite unimpressed.

"Can you not try to look the part that is now yours?" she demanded. "Where is the cloak trimmed in ermine? The ruby encrusted scepter? The crown with the diamonds and emeralds wrested from the mountains of Fhir Mhoil where dwarves vie for the mere right to gaze at the map in the hall of Assyent and guess where the truest gems might be mined? I do not see it upon your head."

"'Tis under his bed."

Gil looked at Mehar in astonishment as she walked past him without so much as a smile. She called to Fleet, clicked to his horse, then led off Tiare and Douglass's horses toward the stables as well. He stood there now without excuse. And as tempting as it was to leave those guests standing before his doors, he knew he couldn't.

"A better welcome we certainly could have expected," Douglass groused pointedly.

"I've been a bit busy," Gil said, then gestured toward his front door. "If you'll follow me, I'll see you settled."

"In heaven only knows what sort of unacceptable accommodations," Tiare said with a heavy sigh.

Gil said nothing more as he led them into the palace. It was almost overwhelmingly tempting to tell them to go find lodging elsewhere—say, in the next kingdom. He tried to lay his finger on a good reason why he couldn't, but the only one he dredged up was that his mother would have been unimpressed by his hospitality and sorely disappointed in his aforementioned comportment and attention to duty. He didn't think that was a good reason, but perhaps it was the best he could do for the moment.

Besides, it was his betrothed he led down the passageway to the great hall.

Damn her anyway.

He tried to concentrate on what was being spewed at him but all he could think about was the fact that he really wished he were out in the stables, inviting Mehar of Angesand to sit whilst he tended their beasts, not showing Tiare of Penrhyn her chamber and listening to her tell him how both it and he were lacking.

After waiting for his guests to be settled, he led them to the hall so they might soothe their complaining stomachs.

"Is there no supper waiting for us?" Tiare asked, aghast.

Hay, straw, a few oats. If those were good enough for their horses, wouldn't they be good enough for Tiare and her sire? Gil closed his eyes, took a deep breath to shore up his dwindling supply of patience, then ushered them toward the table. "If you'll take your ease, I'll see what Cook has on the fire."

"Do you have no servants?" Tiare asked, still quite unhappily surprised. "And your hall—has no one polished the floors? Scrubbed the walls? Cleaned the tapestries? It looks as if all your people have been on holiday for weeks instead of seeing to their tasks."

He would obviously have to work on that hasty spell he'd thrown together and add a bit of cleaning to it. He was actually quite impressed that the place looked as good as it did and that no one had suffered any cuts or bruises as the stones had replaced themselves in mostly their proper places.

"I'll go put the whip to the sweepers," he said dryly.

"I should hope so," Tiare said. She dusted her chair off, accompanied by several noises of disgust, then sat down and looked around expectantly.

Alcuin appeared at Gil's side. He glared at Tiare and Tiare returned the glare. Gil thought it wise to excuse himself before he found himself in the crossfire.

"I'll see how supper is progressing," he said, making Tiare and her father a low bow, then escaping to the kitchens, wondering why he'd ever let his father talk him into having anything to do with the woman he quickly left behind him. He had supposed at the time that since he had to wed, he might as well please his father in his choice. Penrhyn was as good as any for the making of alliances.

Then again, so was Angesand.

He wondered if Mehar knew how very rich her father was, or how very powerful. It was no secret that Robert considered himself ruler of his own small kingdom on the edge of the southern forests. Mehar obviously knew little about her sire's reputation, else she never would have dared flee her home. The number of men Angesand could command with a mere frown was impressive. Why they hadn't come thundering down the road right after her, Gil didn't know. All the more reason to keep a close eye on her.

Though to what end, he couldn't have said, given that he wasn't free.

Would that he were.

He walked through the kitchens. "Penrhyn's here," he said, hurrying on his way. He heard something hit the wall behind him and surmised Cook had thrown a pot lid at him. "That could have killed me!" he bellowed back down the outer passageway.

"Save me cooking a wedding feast!" came the response.

True enough, he supposed.

He walked along his preferred path that led to his preferred location and found that his steps were not as light as he might have otherwise wished. He slowed to a stop. What was he doing, going to find a woman he couldn't have? Thinking to pass any more time with a woman who couldn't be his?

He put his hand on the door to the stable, stood there for a very long moment whilst he wrestled with his duty, then sighed and turned away.

That was when he heard Fleet scream in anger.

He flung open the door and sprinted forward, coming suddenly to a skidding halt, sending straw and dirt scattering everywhere.

A man stood over Mehar, the dagger in his upraised arm gleaming wickedly in the lamplight. Fleet was crashing against the stall door.

Mehar was frozen, a look of complete terror on her face.

Gil cleared his throat. "Excuse me," he said politely. "I think you're trespassing."

The man turned, then snarled out a vicious curse.

Gil felt something akin to pity for the fool. If he'd had a better fortnight, he might have been kinder.

As it was, he suspected the man might pay for quite a few things that hadn't been his doing.

Chapter Five

In Which Mehar Loses Her Heart in a Most Thorough Manner...

Mehar sat on the floor and shivered. It wasn't just from the terror she felt, though that was certainly flowing through her abundantly. Nay, it was that she was watching Gilraehen the Fey prove all the rumors about himself to be true.

She'd come to the stables, removed the gear from Gil's horse, and put him in his stall. She'd done the same to Fleet, without lingering over his grooming as she usually did. A pity she hadn't. If she'd still been at her work, she would have had something in her hand, something she could have used as a weapon. As it was, she had turned from Fleet's stall only to face a man of grim and evil mien who announced himself with nothing more than a drawn dagger pointed at her. She'd tried to flee past him only to find herself thrown to the ground.

She'd tried desperately to draw a spell of protection around herself, but she'd forgotten the words, forgotten how Gil had taught her to weave the words, forgotten everything but her fear and the knowledge that she was going to die. Either at this man's hand or Hagoth's, it was inevitable.

And then Gil had appeared.

He had brought no sword, but apparently he hadn't needed one. He'd fought the bounty hunter with his hands alone.

Or with one hand, rather.

Mehar was torn between watching his good hand as it now made a casual motion that sent the man's knife flying, and staring in horrified pity at his withered hand as he held it to his side.

It wasn't the first time she'd seen that other hand. She had seen it after he'd worked the magic that had so suddenly and completely put the palace to rights. She'd seen it as he'd leaned wearily against his horse, his ruined hand tangled in its mane. He'd stood there, stripped of all the illusion she now knew he was capable of. A powerful magic, his, if he could maintain it about his person so easily.

The company from Penrhyn had obviously marked nothing amiss. Perhaps they'd been too busy complaining about whatever seemed to fall beneath their critical eyes. Mehar had counted herself lucky to have escaped before they turned upon her like ravaging dogs.

"Think ye can best me?" the bounty hunter demanded angrily, trying to lay his hands on Gil and finding it somehow quite impossible. Wherever he lunged, Gil seemed not to be; wherever he struck, Gil was no longer there. "Use both hands, damn ye, and give me a fair fight."

Mehar found that her breath had returned, and with it a bit of her courage. "He's Prince Gilraehen, you know. He doesn't need two hands."

The man faltered and came to be standing quite still for a moment before he made the usual signs of ward she'd always seen accompany any talk about the eldest prince. Mehar couldn't help but laugh, though she supposed she might have been doing the same thing if she hadn't passed the last few days in Gil's company and found him to be an ordinary sort of fellow.

When he wasn't about his magic, that was.

She looked again at the bounty hunter to judge his reaction to it all. He looked appropriately horrified and was still frantically making signs of ward against Gil.

And then, quite suddenly, the man wasn't there. In his place was a large, quite ugly, quite immobile spider. Gil, his breathing just the slightest bit labored, looked at her.

There was a wildness in his eyes that she might have feared, had it been directed at her.

"He's yours," he said.

"That's a very big spider," she said.

He lifted a single finger in the slightest of gestures and the spider shrank to something that could have easily been squashed under her shoe. Mehar looked down, then took a deep breath.

"I suppose something larger than he might eat him." She looked at him. "Do you think?"

He waited. When she said no more, he stepped forward and ground the spider under his boot.

And so ended the life of one of her father's ruffians.

Gil held out his hand and pulled her up onto her feet. From there, it was all too easy to go into his arms. She closed her eyes, breathed in his wildness, and felt it sink into her soul.

Far, far too easy, indeed.

"Are you hurt?" he asked quietly.

She shook her head and shivered. "I'm not, but that is thanks to you. I wanted to use the spell, but I couldn't remember how to make it work."

"It takes time."

"I don't have time."

He ran his hand gently over her hair. "You have me to look after you until you master what you must. You have time."

She lingered for another exquisite moment, then pulled away and took a step backward. She didn't have him; there was a woman inside the castle who would make certain of that. And she certainly couldn't ask him for his time when it was promised elsewhere. She looked up at him, into his fell eyes, and wished things were different.

If she'd had her sisters' beauty, her mother's grace, her father's blessing and riches...

But how could she have ever expected the future king of Neroche to look at her and see past her stained fingers and flyaway hair?

"Thank you for the aid," she said, suddenly finding it easier to look down at his boots than up at his face. "I think I am unprepared for this."

"We all are, in the beginning," he said.

She looked up at that. "Trading the mage lessons for pasties," she said in mock disgust, trying desperately to find a lighter tone. "You are a terrible liar."

He smiled and the dimple in his cheek almost felled her where she stood. "I didn't lie. I did take him all number of treats, for then he would let me from my lessons early."

"Well, you seemed to have managed in spite of that."

He sobered slightly. "The magic in the blood cannot be denied. As you have found."

"You're hedging. You led me astray with that story, diverted me from finding out who you really were. And that business about your name," she said with a snort. "Gilford, indeed."

"It seemed worth the lie, to have you see me differently. I wanted the novel experience of being just Gil the Ordinary," he said, reaching out to tuck a strand of hair behind her ear. "With you."

"And how was it?"

He smiled at her. "Much like you are. Breathtaking."

She stared at him, not wanting to breathe, not wanting to break whatever unbreakable spell he was weaving about them both. He took her hand, casually, as if he feared she would bolt if she realized what he was doing.

She could only look at him, mute, and labor under the thoughts that clamored for her attention: that she might have fallen in love years ago with the prince who had used her mourning gift so thoroughly; that she might have even more fond feelings for the golden peasant she'd passed the past several days with; that she might be becoming unsettlingly enamored with the man who so casually taught her wizard's speak and rode like a demon through palace gardens and over fallen statues, and ragged hedges.

And to think all those men were merely facets of none other than Gilraehen the Fey, Prince of Neroche.

King of Neroche, now.

She wished that she'd known it from the first; she never would have allowed herself any feelings for him at all if she had.

"I *will* keep you safe," he said quietly.

She shook her head. She would make her way alone soon enough. It was what she had planned on from the start, after all. There was no reason to change that just because she'd found her heart involved in something she hadn't planned on. Magic was her goal and she would just have to continue her search for someone who could teach it to her.

She realized, with a start, that tears were coursing down her cheeks.

Gil put his arms around her and pulled her close again. "Mehar, I'm sorry," he whispered. "I'm sorry."

She shook her head, but found nothing to say. She merely stood there in his arms and contemplated the apology she would have to offer for soaking his shirt.

A throat cleared itself from a safe distance behind them. "Gil? They grow restless inside and you know I cannot satisfy them."

"In a moment," Gil said. "I'll be there in a moment."

"Well," Alcuin said, "I wouldn't let myself be caught in the stables thus were I you. No offense, Mehar."

Mehar pulled away from Gil, then pulled her sleeve across her eyes. "Just trying to wash up a bit," she said. "Didn't have any decent water to hand."

Alcuin grunted but said nothing.

Gil dragged his good hand through his hair. "I have to go."

"Aye, you do." She put her shoulders back. "Sorry for the tears. I'm not used to the price on my head, you see."

He was looking at her, she could sense, but she couldn't meet his eyes. Whatever he felt, whatever she might have imagined he felt, he was still set to wed with the Princess of Penrhyn. Even if he hadn't been, that was no guarantee he would turn his clear eye her way.

"Alcuin, watch over her," he said with a sigh. "Who knows what other kind of filth is lurking about. Apparently, my defenses aren't what they should be, but I don't dare do more."

Alcuin steered him back toward the stable doors. "Go. I'll keep watch over her. And I'll entertain her with all sorts of unsavory things about you after you've gone."

"Sounds treasonous," Mehar said, trying to smile.

Gil muttered something under his breath, shot her a final searing look that made her shiver, then turned on his heel, and walked swiftly from the stables. Mehar looked at Alcuin, who, for once, didn't curse at her. Instead, he handed her a coin.

"Take it back," he said. "If I'd known what you were about, I would have given you the hare freely, and caught you another."

"You're too kind."

"I pity you," he said simply. "Gil, of all people. Don't you know he has more bad habits than I have curses? Now, if you were to cast your eye *my* way, you would find a man of truly impressive lineage, impeccable manners, and diverting antics."

"But I haven't cast my eye his way," she protested.

He stared at her so long that she finally had to look away.

"Harrumph," he grunted. "Poor wench. Well, we'd best be about some sort of training for you. *Never let magic rule when a dagger will do* is my motto."

"Do you have no magic of your own?"

"None that I'll admit to," he said. "Besides, I'm fonder of my blade than all that whispering and muttering under my breath. Bring that dagger lying fallow over there and we'll make for the chicken coop. It's empty and no one will look for us there. Especially no one from Penrhyn, if our luck holds."

She followed him from the stable silently—silently because he seemed to have as many words to hand as he did foul oaths and he seemed determined to talk her to death.

"Thank you," she said, when he finally paused for a few good breaths.

"For that?" he asked, his eyes quite devoid of guile. "You don't really like him anyway, do you? He snores, you know. And he doesn't bathe on long marches. I think you'd be far better off with someone not so afeared of a harmless bit of soap. Take me, for instance. Come along, woman, and I will list my virtues for you. That will occupy the whole of the afternoon."

"Will there be another list on the morrow?"

He smiled, and Gil's dimple showed from his cheek as well. "Of course. I have a quite exhaustive supply."

"Heaven help me."

"Aye, you'll say that as well, when I find you a sword."

"I know where to find a sword," she said.

Alcuin looked at her sharply. "Is it keeping company with a crown?"

"It might be."

He grunted. "Well, then you'd best keep a good eye on both. And we'll go over that spell of protection again, the one Gil taught you this morning. Even I can manage that one in moments of strain, Mehar. Don't know why you can't."

But he patted her companionably on the back as he said it, and she knew she had a friend, at least for a while. She let out her breath slowly. She could do this; she could remain at the castle and learn what she needed to, then be on her way.

And then she would pray she never would have to see Gilraehen the Fey again.

Her heart wouldn't survive it.

Chapter Six

In Which Gilraehen Finds That Serving Sup-
per Can Be a Perilous Undertaking…

Several endless hours later, Gil stood in the shadows of the
kitchen herb garden and watched Mehar go at a helpless bush
with his father's sword.

It was, he had to admit, a novel sight.

Fortunately for the shrub, she didn't seem to be able to get it
and the sword within the same arc, but she made a valiant effort.
She swung, she heaved, she spun.

She landed quite firmly upon her backside.

She looked around quickly, as if to make certain no one had seen
her, but Gil knew he was too far in the shadows to be seen even despite a very full moon, so he didn't worry. Besides, he wasn't laughing. He remembered quite well his first lessons with the sword—a
sword that he later realized had been purposely too heavy for him.
Perhaps Master Wemmit had been trying to teach him humility.
He'd certainly never learned the like as a part of more otherworldly
lessons. Nay, sword mastery had come dear, and he prized it the
more for the effort.

Mehar might as well, in time, though he couldn't imagine what she might be thinking to do with such a skill. There were shield-maidens in his father's kingdom, he supposed, but they were seldom made such without grave necessity. A brother, a father, a lover wounded and in need of protection—those were the things that drove a woman to master a blade and bend it to her purposes.

His hand ached suddenly, and then his heart, followed quite hard by a flush of shame. To think that she might have seen his hand he could stomach; that she might want to aid him was moving; that she might have him enough in her heart that she would tramp about in the mud in the middle of the night to pay for that skill so she might protect him made him, by turns, humbled and astonished that he could be so foolish. She was not there for him; she was there for herself.

He wished with all his heart that she needn't be.

Damn that Tiare of Penrhyn and damn him for having agreed to endure her waspish tongue.

Mehar had, whilst he'd been about his torturous thoughts, picked herself up, taken a firmer grasp on the king's sword, and proceeded to try to demonstrate to it who was in charge.

A goodly while later, when the moon had moved quite a bit more toward the middle of the night, even Gil had to admit that said soul was not her.

He watched her as she sighed heavily, jammed his father's sword into the ground, then turned her attentions elsewhere. She fetched her mother's book and studied a page for a few minutes. She put the book aside, then wove a spell of protection quite beautifully over her chosen bush. Gil was tempted to add his own charm to the shrubbery, but refrained. Let the victory be hers.

She retrieved his father's sword and hacked at the bush with all her strength.

The sword clove it in twain.

Gil held his breath.

Leaves had scattered, branches had split and cracked, and blossoms were lying on the ground.

Or so it seemed.

Then, slowly, the ruin dissipated, and the bush resumed its proper form.

She laughed.

He smiled so hard, tears sprang to his eyes.

Might the stars in the heavens and the pitiless faeries in their sparkling palaces look upon him with mercy, he was lost.

Mehar examined her handiwork another moment or two, then took her book and his sire's sword and trudged back to the house. He watched her go and wished he'd never been born the prince, never agreed to wed Tiare, never given his heart where it couldn't go. If only he could change the present... He leaned back against the stone of the palace wall and wished for a miracle.

Unfortunately, given the lack of miracles in his life so far, he didn't hold out much hope.

Eventually, he pushed away from the wall and headed back to the hall himself. Maybe if hope wouldn't be with him, luck might, and he would avoid any unpleasant encounters with any of his future in-laws until he had his treasonous heart under control.

He thought about seeking a bed, but found himself suddenly standing before the door to the chamber of records. It didn't matter to him, really, who Mehar's forbearers were. He would have loved her if she'd been a thief or a princess, poor fool that he was. But since he was where he was, there was no sense in not seeing what a little look into Tagaire's impossibly cluttered chamber might yield. He pushed the door open, took a deep breath, then sneezed heartily.

He picked his way around stacks of papers, teetering piles of books, and perilously positioned inkwells. Apparently, his spell of restoration had worked all too well inside Tagaire's chamber—taking it back to its former state of glorious disarray.

He spent the rest of the night turning manuscript pages and wishing for better light than the weak magelight he dared conjure up. A candle didn't bear thinking on; he had visions of the entire chamber catching fire due to a stray spark and that kept him from looking for any suitable wicks.

Dawn had broken and the sun was well into his rise toward midmorning before Gil made his way, bleary-eyed but much enlightened, toward the kitchens. He'd found Elfine of Angesand's name entered neatly into Tagaire's books, and thereby knew her claim to a mighty magic. Her line was pure, going back to Isobail of Camanaë, who was the mightiest of her kind in the days when those with gifts had been assembled together and their places decided upon. What would Mehar do, if she knew? Wilt under the pressure or rise to great heights because of it?

He would tell her, eventually, when he thought it would serve her. For now, his curiosity satisfied, he suspected that what would serve him best was a hearty breakfast.

He walked into the kitchens to find Cook in high dudgeon. She banged and clattered and cursed loudly. And that was just when she saw him.

"Have they been awake long?" he asked politely.

He ducked to miss the flying spoon, then loitered with his hip against the worktable whilst she made ready a substantial meal.

"I don't think you've ever fed me this well," he remarked.

"I won't be feeding you at all if you don't send them on their way," Cook threatened.

"And how am I to do that?" he asked.

"A finger gesturing toward the front door might do."

He refrained from comment. For all he knew, one of Tiare's spies was lurking behind the flour barrel, waiting for just such an admission of agreement, whereupon the scout would immediately repair to his mistress and tell the full tale. Gil would then find himself begging pardon from a furious Princess of Penrhyn.

He shuddered at the thought.

So instead, he waited, and while he waited, he examined Mehar's lineage and that of his own and speculated on the children such a union might produce. A fruitless and dangerous speculation, to be sure, but he hadn't slept well in a very long time and his poor wits were at their worst.

Such unhealthy contemplation took him through the rest of Cook's grudging meal preparations and on into the great hall where he struggled to carry several dishes in his arms. He wasn't very good at it, given that his maimed hand was of use for little besides trying to keep the plates balanced on his other arm, but he was the king, after all, and not a page, so perhaps it didn't matter what he dropped. Hopefully he would be better at juggling the affairs of his realm than he was at juggling plates of meat and bowls of sauce.

Dour Douglass was already seated and Tiare was preparing to sit when he reached the high table. He started to set down his burdens when Tiare set up a screech so piercing that he dropped everything in surprise.

"Damnation, woman," he exclaimed. "What are you—"

She only made more shrill noises that left him wanting to cover his ears. He looked about him in alarm, half expecting to see an army of trolls marching in to make a breakfast of him and his guests.

But there was nothing in the hall.

Nothing but him, Tiare, and her father.

And then he realized, quite suddenly, what was amiss.

In his haste to see to Tiare's comfort and make the meal presentable, he'd neglected to make himself presentable as well. Tiare was pointing to his maimed hand with a look of complete horror on her face.

"I will not wed with *that*," she howled.

"The dirt will wash off him," her father said placidly. "Look you, he's already cleaner than he was yesterday."

"Look at his *hand*, Father," she cried.

Douglass had his look, then shrugged. "New scars. Freshly healed. They'll fade in time. Lost the use of it as well, lad?"

Gil put his hand behind his back and inclined his head. "For the moment. It will heal."

"It will heal," Douglass agreed dismissively. "Come, Tiare, sit.

Perhaps there is drinkable wine in this place today. Used to be. Can't say what we'll find now that young Gilraehen is master here. Any wine left below, boy, or have your men sucked it all up?"

Tiare dug in her heels. "I will *not* wed with him," she announced. "I simply will not."

"Aye, you will," Douglass said.

"You'll have to bind me and bring me to the altar. And even then I will not agree, no matter the times you beat me, or stick me with a blade. I will not. I simply will *not*." She gave Gil a withering look. "I will not wed with a dirty, bedraggled oaf who is so weak he leaves his hall to be overrun by ruffians and so feeble he can't guard even his own hand. Are you to wed me to this, Father? This man who cannot even see to himself? This man who likely left his sire to die on the field so he could escape?"

At that moment, though he suspected it was just a rewishing of things he had wished so many times he'd lost count, Gil heartily wished that she would find someone else to ply her flaying tongue upon and leave him in peace.

Douglass eyed him with disfavor. "Bloody hell, lad, did you hear that? Wouldn't put up with that kind of talk myself."

"And what is it you suggest I do, my lord?" Gil asked. "Beat her?"

"I would."

"I wouldn't."

"Well," Douglass said in disgust, "there is where you've gone wrong."

"I don't care what either of you thinks," Tiare said archly. "I will *not* wed with a man of his... his... *ilk*," she spat. "Bad enough that he's mad as a loon and fey as a sprite. That he should be so... so..." Words seemed to fail her at this point. She glared at Gil as if his injury and all the other unsettling things that surrounded him were entirely his fault. "I will not wed with a sorcerer." She turned her glare on her sire. "You cannot make me, Father."

"You'll do what I tell you —"

"I'll kill myself first. See if I don't."

Dour Douglass looked unimpressed.

"He has nothing to give you anyway," Tiare said scornfully. "Look you at his hall. If he could afford my bride price, I would be greatly surprised."

Gil imagined she would be surprised by a great many things, but he refrained from saying as much.

"I have to agree with her about the bride price," Douglass said. "You cannot have the gel for free, and you can't take her dowry then turn about and give it back to me as payment for her. You'll have to buy her with aught of your own, and it doesn't look as if you have aught of your own to spare. At least nothing of this world," he added.

He looked at Gil and Gil supposed it was only vast amounts of self-control that kept the man from making some sign of ward against him.

"And then there are the rumors surrounding your father's demise," Douglass continued. "Those are above and beyond the rumors that surround your own self. And I've heard aught about darkness and danger in the north and east, fell, unwholesome things that are coming your way. Perhaps 'tis well that my daughter not be near you, if that is the case."

Gil blinked in surprise. "Are you casting me aside, my lord king?"

"Aye," Douglass said without hesitation. "But serve me some of those fine-looking victuals first, boy. What you can scrape back onto a plate, of course." He cast Tiare a quick look before he relieved Gil of the platter he had just picked up and retrieved his own meal from what lay scattered on the table.

For herself, Tiare seemed more interested in fleeing the hall than in shoring up her strength.

Gil wondered what it was he would do without Tiare's dowry of brencara. He gave that some thought as he sat on the edge of the table and swung his leg back and forth. He continued to ponder the problem as Dour Douglass plowed through all the victuals he could manage, burped heartily in kingly fashion, then slapped something down at Gil's elbow before he nodded to him and left the hall.

Gil looked down at the small pouch. He opened it, then laughed to himself. Crushed bits of brencara lay therein, surely enough to serve him should he need it in the near future. Perhaps Douglass felt sorry for him; perhaps he felt sorry for himself. Perhaps he had his eye on a richer prize than the kingdom of Neroche. Gil didn't care. For himself, he felt nothing but relief.

Immense, soul-searing relief.

In fact, he was so relieved, he walked around the table, sat himself down, and set to his own breakfast with vigor and a light heart. He ate, chortled, ate some more, and contemplated how he might arrange his future to suit himself now that he was free.

Then he looked up.

Mehar had just walked into his hall. She hesitated, looked about her, then walked over to the table.

"What happened?" she asked. "The Princess of Penrhyn fair ran me over in her haste to reach her chamber. Did the meal not suit her?"

"*I* didn't suit her."

She blinked. "You didn't?"

"I didn't."

She brushed crumbs off the table and sat sideways on its edge so she could look at him. "What are you saying?"

"I'm saying she cast me aside."

"But why would she do that?" Mehar asked. "You're the king, for pity's sake."

He slipped his damaged hand under the table before he thought better of it. Perhaps Mehar shared Tiare's revulsion. "Well," he said finally, "apparently the crown didn't make up for my other flaws."

"I understand from Alcuin that you have many."

"He has more. Come, sit, and I'll tell you of them while you eat." He helped himself to a bit more veg under sauce. "Cook never makes this for me. I should ask her to."

She came around the table to sit next to him. "You eat like a man in a great deal of anguish."

"I imagine I feel much as you felt when you fled your home on that winged steed of yours."

"Happy, happy, happy," Mehar murmured.

"Aye, quite," he agreed. He didn't look at her, for he wasn't sure he wanted to look for more in her eyes than he might see.

But he sat next to her just the same and felt happier than he had in days.

He was free.

And he was king.

And he supposed that since his former bride didn't want him anymore, he might be free to wed where he willed—and if that meant looking toward a woman with a price on her head and a hand with beasts that even Angesand himself would admire, then so be it.

"How much would that bounty your sire wanted for you be, do you suppose?" he asked, absently toying with his knife and watching her from under his eyebrows.

"That depends," she said, helping herself to his ale, "on how much of this he'd been drinking, how long his ire had burned—and how fiercely—and how light his purse was feeling."

He shook his head. Angesand bred magical steeds in his stables and grew gold in his garden, or so the tales said. The man was also notoriously stingy, and exacted exorbitant, though quite deserved prices for his horseflesh. Gil shuddered to think how high a price Angesand would have put on his irritation with Mehar.

Though it was a price Gil would gladly pay. As well as the bride price and whatever it would take to satisfy the jilted bridegroom. He had wealth enough, assuming the vaults under the palace hadn't been plundered. He promised himself a good look in the treasury the first chance he had.

"Who was your betrothed?" he asked. No sense in not knowing

all the damage at once. A pity Tagaire wasn't still alive. Along with the realm's genealogy, he kept a running tally of who was betrothed to whom, the odds of the union being finalized, and the possibilities of decent children to come. When Mehar didn't answer right away, he supposed that perhaps she might not be eager to say, perhaps for shame that such a man might be less than worthy.

"Hagoth," she said finally. "And no doubt he's put a price on my head as well."

"Hagoth?" he echoed, dumbfounded. Hagoth was notorious for choosing young, exquisite brides with vast sums of money to their names and accomplishments to match. "Hagoth," he repeated. "I wouldn't have thought—"

"I know," she interrupted. "Me, of all people." She rose suddenly. "I think I have horses to tend. By your leave, my liege?"

And with that, she turned and walked away.

He stood up. "I didn't mean... that is, I never meant to imply..."

She turned at the doorway. "Don't you have business of the realm to attend to?" she asked briskly.

He paused, considered trying to explain himself, then caught a full view of her glare. He winced. Perhaps the kitchens were the safest place for him at present. "I suppose there are always dishes to wash," he conceded.

She didn't laugh. Instead, she curtseyed to him with all the grace of any of the young, exquisite ingénues who came to present themselves to him, and left the hall.

"Damn," he said to no one in particular.

He almost went after her, but he suspected that anything he might say would go unlistened-to. Perhaps if he gave her time to cool her temper, he might attempt an apology later. So, as penance, he gathered platters and forks, then made his way to where the washing tub resided.

He contemplated his apology as he prepared to be about his task. He could offer to teach her magery. Not just the reading of her mother's book, but the whole business. Spells, changings, the long and illustrious oral tradition that made one anxious to go back out and work with the sword. That might take a very long time. Perhaps years. And perhaps at some point during those years, she might grow to have fond feelings for him.

And perhaps he would learn to check what he planned to say before he said it and avoid any more of the kind of looks he'd received from her after he'd expressed in not so many words his doubt about Hagoth's choice.

Damn it anyway.

Soon, he was deep into his work, his head full of visions of himself with his newly acquired perspicacious and proper tongue contributing to a very happy and unoffended Mehar of Angesand. He had just finished envisioning how she would receive his proposal of marriage when he looked up from the scrubbing of his pots to see his two younger brothers walk into the kitchen, just as they'd done countless times over countless years, seeking something to filch before supper.

"Well," Lanrien said with a laugh, "here we find our good King of Neroche. Up to his elbows in suds."

Tirran laughed as well, snatching a hot cake off the cooling racks and cursing as he juggled it in the air. "He's no fool when it comes to filling his belly or locating the most drinkable ale."

Gil stared at the two men who were currently pestering Cook for things to eat and thought his heart might burst. They were battered and bruised, with rags wrapped about various parts of their forms, but they were whole. Tirran, his dark hair mussed and his bright blue eyes twinkling, looked as if he'd just come in from a ride. Lanrien, fair-haired like their dam, with deep green eyes that held secrets he didn't often share, looked worse for the wear, as if the journey home had been more difficult than he cared to admit. But they were home. Gil could scarce believe it.

They soon left off tormenting Cook and turned to him. He was quite happy for a bucket of suds beneath his hands. It made the tears that fell into it as his brothers hugged him much less noticeable than they would have been had they been dripping with great splats onto the floor.

"You great idiots," Gil said finally, dragging his sleeve across his eyes, "where have you been?"

Tirran shrugged. "Scouting."

"We supposed you didn't have the lads for it," Lanrien added, "what with only Alcuin at your heels."

Gil looked at them unflinchingly. "I ran."

Lanrien returned the look. "We did as well. We had no choice. At least you destroyed most of his army as you left."

"Aye, we just scurried around the side and wished you the best," Tirran agreed cheerfully.

"So I see by the condition of your clothes and yourselves," Gil said dryly.

"Well, at least your hands are clean for the tending of our hurts," Lanrien said pragmatically. "Though you aren't really much on the healing part of it all, are you?"

Gil scowled. "You would think I was the only one in this keep capable of muttering a spell. Why didn't you work on each other?"

"Didn't want to attract attention," Tirran said easily. "And you know we haven't any decent magic. Not for that kind of thing. And, since we haven't bled to death yet, waiting a few more moments won't hurt. Cook, my love, what is it you're creating in that fine copper pot? It smells like heaven."

"It's lunch for Penrhyn and his get," said Cook tartly, "so keep your grubby paws out of it. Your Highness," she added with a nod. "I'll just taste —"

Gil laughed. *His brothers were alive.* Somehow, that made it all more bearable. He shook water off his hands, reached for a towel, then realized his hand wasn't working. Still.

Silence fell. He looked at his brothers, realizing what they'd seen. He put his hand behind his back. "'Tis nothing."

"Gil," Lanrien said in a low voice, "what happened to you?"

"I put my hand into a fire and scorched it. Which is what will happen to you if you're not careful with Cook's pot. And Cook, Penrhyn and his get have departed."

She looked at him hopefully. "For good?"

"For good."

Cook looked pleased. His brothers looked shocked. For himself, he could only smile.

"Come, lads, and let us repair to the hall where we can talk peacefully. We've much to discuss. Did you bring anyone with you, or is it just you two who wafted back to the palace like a bad smell?"

"Ingle the smith," Lanrien said, "and Tagaire as well."

"In truth?" Gil asked, surprised.

"He wields a mighty pen," Tirran said, chewing industriously on something else he'd poached from Cook's table. "Poked several lads with it that I saw. And there are a few others coming along shortly who might be necessary to the running of the keep."

"Then let's have a parley," Gil suggested. "But later, after you've eaten. Follow me and bring food with you."

His brothers followed, and, fortunately for them, chose to make no more comments. He wasn't sure he could have borne any more discussion of his wound, or how it might come to bear on his kingship.

Or on his ability to weave the spells necessary to keep that kingship intact.

He sat down at the table, grateful beyond measure for their companionship and not a little surprised at how he'd grieved unknowingly for its lack. He watched his siblings eat as if they'd been starved for weeks and was content.

Or at least he was until the questions began.

"What of Penrhyn?" Tirran demanded.

Gil shrugged. "She decided she didn't want me."

"Tiare pitched you?" Lanrien asked in astonishment. "What'd you do to her, Gil, tell her that her face matched her wine?"

He shook his head with a smile. "She didn't care for the new look of my paw."

"Daft wench," Tirran said, shaking his head. "At least you aren't weeping over it."

"I'll survive."

"Any new prospects?" Lanrien asked, studying his brother with a grave smile. "Vast armies of lassies of all ages coming to vie for the attentions of the new king?"

"Nay."

Tirran leaned forward. "Then why are you so bloody cheerful? Gil, the future of the realm! The continuation of your line, an heir for the throne!" He waggled his eyebrows. "Think on your duty, brother."

Gil thought about that duty and decided it was perhaps time to see to it. He cuffed Tirran affectionately on the back of the head and rose. "If that's the case, then our parley can wait. I've business in the stables."

"Don't tell us you've fallen for a stable wench," Tirran said in disbelief.

"A horse breeder's daughter, actually."

They were silent long enough for him to gain the passageway leading to the kitchens.

"Who?" Lanrien bellowed.

"Gil, wait!" Tirran shouted.

He continued on his way, smiling. His brothers were alive. Could his life improve?

He suspected it could, so he quickened his pace.

He entered the stabled and paused in the shadows where he could watch Mehar stroking Fleet's nose. Whatever else might be happening to his realm, whatever horrors awaited him in the future, whatever deep waters he might need to swim in before he reached peace and stability, he didn't care if he could just stand there and look at her for a moment or two more.

For he was, as he had noted earlier, free, and he was the king.

Which surely meant that he could choose his bride where he willed.

He stood there for so long, thinking on that happy prospect, that he failed to notice when exactly it was that Mehar turned to look at him. She was leaning on the stall door and staring at him solemnly.

"My liege?" she queried. "Did your meal not sit well with you?"

"Best one I've had in years," he admitted with a smile. "I was just now lost in thought."

"The weightier matters of the realm?"

"I was considering choosing a bride, actually."

Had her smile faltered? He looked closely, searching for a sign that it had. Unfortunately, all he could decide was that perhaps a bit of dust had floated up and tickled her nose.

"I wish you good fortune," she said, sounding perfectly content that he might be about his choosing and not in the least bit interested that he turn that choosing in her direction.

He decided to take matters into his own hands. It was one of his father's most useful traits and he'd inherited a goodly quantity of it. He walked across the hay-strewn floor, paused a pair of steps away from her, and assumed a like pose of leaning with his elbow atop the railing. He stood there and admired her dark gray eyes, her riotous hair that had yet again escaped her plait, and her hands that were cracked, worn, and wearing a fine layer of dirt and other stable-ish kinds of things.

Ah, but what a woman this one was.

Indeed, he was so intent on admiring her that he completely forgot his hand until he saw her gaze fall upon it. But she only looked at it, then looked up at him, neither pity nor disgust on her face. Gil straightened and put his hand behind his back.

"I came to see if you might be willing to aid me," he said formally, all thoughts of proposing a union suddenly gone from his mind. Angesand's daughter she was, and therefore she might have her standards in a husband. King though he might have been, he certainly had flaws enough.

"Aid you?" she repeated. "How, my liege?"

"You called me Gil this morning."

"I'm feeling formal."

"I'm not wearing a crown."

She smiled briefly. "Then how may I aid you, Gilraehen the Fey?"

He wondered why the sound of his name from a woman's lips without a charm or ward attached should please him so much. He dragged his wandering thoughts back to the present with an effort. "I came to discuss wedding you, but perhaps you would prefer to learn a bit of healing so you might see to my brothers."

She blinked.

He did as well, when he realized what he'd said. He was tempted to curse his tongue—for he'd certainly intended a more flowery proposal, one in which he laid out a thorough inventory of his virtues—but perhaps his tongue had things aright where he didn't.

Then Mehar laughed. He supposed he should have been affronted by it, but he couldn't seem to muster up any kind of serious frown.

"Wed me?" she echoed. "Who, you?"

"Is the thought so ridiculous?"

She finally had to sit down, the thought was apparently so ridiculous. He did find an appropriately displeased expression, but that only made her laugh the harder. He finally sat down next to her on an unassuming bale of hay and waited until her mirth had subsided. She sighed finally, wiping the tears from her eyes.

"Wouldn't that be something?" she asked. "Me, wedding you."

"I cannot decide if I should be insulted or not."

She shook her head. "Nay, my lord, I am surely not high enough for the likes of you."

"I am king," he said loftily. "I can decide who is high enough for me and who isn't. And perhaps you don't realize your father's place in the kingdom. I may have the crown and the title, but his power and wealth are easily equal to mine."

She blinked. "In truth?"

"Mehar, what have you been doing all your life?"

"Weaving upstairs and avoiding royal guests."

He took her hand, then suddenly he saw that hand in another place, weaving a blanket to slip around the shoulders of a young prince who had lost his dam. He saw her with a shuttle in her hand, saw the tears that fell from her eyes as she wove love and pity into the plaid of the cloth that would go around him in the dark of night and bring him ease. He took that hand, that tender hand, and held it against his cheek.

"Your gift," he said. "The mourning cloth."

Tears sprang to her eyes. "You used it."

"Endlessly." He kissed the palm of her hand. "Perhaps 'twas when I first touched it that my heart was given and 'tis only now that the strands of fate have woven us together at last." He smiled at her. "I can be grateful your father was so foresighted as to have hidden you away that you might be mine."

"I'm certain it wasn't for that reason," she said dryly.

He rubbed his thumb over her hand, stained as it was from dye and work, then met her eyes.

"Can you not love me, Mehar with the price on her head?"

She looked down at his hand surrounding hers, then nodded slowly. "I could, Gilraehen of Neroche. But about that price on my head—"

"What will I have to sell?"

"What won't you?"

He laughed. "Tell me of it as we wed."

"My father will be furious when he learns," she warned.

"That I wed you, or that I saved him from having to pay someone to deliver you to him?"

"That he wasn't consulted," she said. "But point out to him the gold it saved him and he'll likely toast you with his finest."

"I'll send Alcuin to him to give him the tidings and let him brave both your sire's wrath and his wine. As for you, will you not come with me and let us be about our business whilst the day is yet young?" He didn't wait for an answer, but pulled her to her feet and along behind him for several paces until she dug in her heels so firmly that he was forced to stop and look at her. "Aye?"

"You've said nothing of your heart, my liege."

"Why do you think I was so relieved to see Tiare go?"

"That's hardly an answer."

He pulled her into his arms, kissed her thoroughly, then looked down at her with a smile. "My heart is full of you, Mehar of Angesand. Is that answer enough? It was full of you the moment I saw you. I've spent a completely inappropriate amount of time over the past several days wishing Tiare of Penrhyn would take herself and her sharp tongue and go home so I could wed where I willed."

"Have you?" she asked wistfully.

"Aye," he said, "I have."

She looked down at her hand in his, then met his gaze. "Then I am content."

He led her back to the hall, content as well. Later that day there would be time to talk to his brothers, to face the heavy reality that was his and now would be Mehar's, but for now, for the next few hours, he would put it aside and be glad of a woman who loved him for himself.

It was indeed enough.

Chapter Seven

*In Which Mehar Solves the Mystery of Her Mother
from a Most Unexpected Source...*

Mehar sat across from her newly made husband near the fire in his grand and glorious hall and wondered if she could possibly manage what it was he asked of her. His brothers sat on either side of him, healed and well, and watching her expectantly. Her healing of them had gone quite well, but admittedly their wounds had been minor ones. She wasn't sure she could take confidence from her experience with them.

Alcuin sat on her right, making noises of impatience that were so distracting she finally had to glare him into silence. Then she took Gil's hand in hers, held it gently between both her own, and looked into his shattered blue eyes. "I don't think this will hurt."

"I daresay it will."

"How can it? My magic is supposed to be a gentle one."

"Aye, that is the rumor, but the truth may be quite a different thing. But I will bear the attempt." He smiled at her briefly, then nodded once, and closed his eyes.

Mehar looked down at his hand; it was red, twisted, laced with angry weals as if he'd thrust it into a fire full of teeth. She traced her

fingers over his skin, felt him shiver. Well, there was no use in waiting. She took a deep breath and started to weave the simple spell of
healing Gil had taught her from her mother's book.

She found it difficult to concentrate. The events of the day, leading up to where she now sat, clamored for her attention. She wasn't
completely convinced that she wouldn't wake and find herself back
in her own cold tower room, buried under blankets that her mother
had wrought, and wishing that her future might be other than it
promised to be.

That morning, after she'd come back to the palace with Gil,
Alcuin had taken her under his wing until all was made ready. His
grumbling had been continual, beginning with his reminding her
that he was but Gil's cousin ("never will see the damned throne myself,") though captain of his army ("never will see one of *those* of my
own either,") dispenser of marital vows ("are you certain you wish
to wed with this oaf here, or did he persuade you unfairly,") and
questionable placer of crowns upon the heads of uncrowned kings
("how does it look on *my* head? Better than Gil's, don't you agree?")
He had concluded with an expectant look she'd laughed at, which
had incited yet another round of grumbling that had taken her
through a hall which had been filled with twinkling lights she hadn't
been able to determine the origin of.

"He is fey, you know," Alcuin had reminded her. "I'd think twice
about wedding him, were I you."

She had known, and she didn't have to think twice. She had
crossed the floor in a gown of Gil's mother's, placed her hand in
the hand of her king, and wed him without so much as a breath of
hesitation.

Gil's hand twitched and she came to herself, realizing that she
had stopped speaking. She looked at him and smiled apologetically.

"Regrets?" he asked.

"Oh, aye," she said with a small laugh. "I'm sure I'll live well
into my old age wishing I'd put my hand down to be crushed un-

der Hagoth's heel instead of into yours to be brought close to your heart."

"Will you listen to that?" Alcuin grumbled to Gil's brothers. "I think the girl likes him, poor wench."

Tirran punched Alcuin in the arm. "You just wish she were yours, but you haven't Gil's charm, so shut up."

"It wasn't his charm," Lanrien offered, "it was his sweet temper and handsome face that so resembles my own handsome face that won him the day."

"Not to mention his murky reputation," Mehar added with a smile at her husband of five hours.

That launched an entirely new discussion of Gil's murky reputation and how that might affect the affairs of the realm in the near future. At least they were talking about something else, and quite loudly, too, so she could concentrate on what she was doing.

When she was finished, she looked critically at Gil's hand and her heart sank. "I don't think there's any change."

"It was a very powerful spell that wrought the damage," he said easily. "It will take a spell equally powerful to fashion the healing. You'll manage it —"

"Let her manage it later," Alcuin interrupted. "Cook is bellowing for hands to carry in the wedding feast." He looked pointed at Gil and found himself cuffed quite enthusiastically by Lanrien.

"Dolt," Lanrien said, "he's the bridegroom."

"And the king," Tirran added.

"Which neither of *you* are," Alcuin groused. "Come help me."

Mehar waited until they'd left before she looked at Gil. "Will he ever show you any deference?"

"He'll muster up a bit of bobbing and scraping when others are about," he assured her. "But other than that, we can count on him treating me as just Gil the Ordinary."

Mehar looked at him, with his terrible beauty, his eyes that contained the shards of sky and water, his face that held secrets she wasn't sure she was ready to know, and thought him anything but ordinary. But she didn't say as much. Instead, she leaned forward and kissed him, easily, as if she'd been doing it all her life—in spite of the fact that the very act of it made her heart feel as if it would never again regain its proper place in her form.

"I suppose," she said pulling back, "that you'll need someone about you to remind you you're merely a man when you begin to take yourself too seriously."

"And you won't?" he asked, cocking his head to one side.

She shook her head. "I am your warp threads, my liege, ever fixed in my affections. Let someone else correct your pattern. My task is to wrap you in peace and comfort, not strip you of it."

He smiled, reached out, and put his hand to her cheek. "I thank you for the safe harbor. Come and sit by me, that we might enjoy that peace."

While we have it, was what she heard him add, though he didn't say it aloud and she suspected he wasn't talking about insults from his cousin. But she sat next to him just the same, cut his meat as if she'd been his page (and that over his vociferous protests,) and listened to Alcuin and his brothers drag out instruments and sing several ballads that she'd never heard, though she was certainly not one for the recognizing of such given her lack of presence in her own father's hall.

After supper, Gil rose. His brothers were conspicuously silent, his cousin as well, until they had been left a safe distance behind. Then all manner of suggestions were called out. Gil stepped past the threshold, uttered a single, sharp command, and the doors slammed shut behind them with a resounding bang.

"Did you shut them in there for the night?" Mehar asked.

"Aye," he said with a superior smile. "I also filled the hall with a collection of terrifying wildlife that will keep them busy for most of the night."

The curses that immediately began to stream out from under the doorway were proof enough of that. Mehar shook her head, put her hand in her love's, and walked with him to the bedchamber he'd given her in the beginning.

And after their night's work was done, she fell asleep in his arms, wrapped in the bit of weaving that she'd once upon a time sent him to ease his heart.

She'd never imagined it might cover them both.

The morning came and brought with it an abrupt end to the peace and quiet she'd wished for, though she wasn't surprised and Gil seemed even less so. She washed and dressed without fuss and walked with him quietly to the great hall where an array of grim-faced men awaited their king.

She looked about the circle at the men who had come uncalled to Gil's need. There were men of Gil's father's house who had straggled back from the battle: Ingle, the steel-smith; Laverock, the apprentice keeper of records; Tagaire, his master; Hirsel, the stable master; and Wemmit the Grim, the sword master. Others sat there as well, men who had no title and no names that they would offer.

Lords of other kinds had come as well, seemingly in the night. A dwarf with piercing black eyes and a long, slender nose sat across from Gil, caressing the curve of a small knife as he listened. There was another man who sat apart, long-fingered like Gil, but shorter in stature and quite old. He had a jolly face, but she sensed something beneath his worn exterior that bespoke great power.

And then off to one side, quite aloof, but so desperately handsome that she could scarce look at him without shielding her eyes, sat a stranger. If the man hadn't reminded her so much of Gil with his aura of power, she might have felt a little disloyal in the way she couldn't seem to stop herself from staring at him. She finally leaned over to whisper to Alcuin who sat next to her, silent and watchful.

"Who is that?" she asked.

He grunted. "Bloody elf. Don't see much of them, as they don't usually leave their gilt-edged halls. They must be worried."

She looked at him. "Are you?"

"Never." He smiled a rather fierce smile. "You haven't seen Gil annoyed. Lothar bested him last time; he won't again. I think Gil took pity on him, in some small fashion, because Lothar is his uncle."

She blinked. "His uncle?"

"His great-grandfather's brother."

"Indeed."

"Second thoughts?" Alcuin asked hopefully.

"None."

"Damn," he whispered, but it was lacking in conviction. "That's why Gil's fey, you know. That magic from Wychweald. He has it a hundredfold by some bit of fate, and that says nothing of what he has from his dam. That magic is something his brothers got little of. You'll notice they aren't exactly over endowed with that look that makes you want to rub your arms and try to get warm."

"Aye, I did notice. Why is that?"

Alcuin shrugged. "Who knows why magic chooses the course it does? Maybe Gil was fated to be king. The lads have enough magic to reign, should it come to that, I suppose—and Lanrien more than Tirran—but it would be a far different kingdom."

She nodded, but found herself distracted by the terrible talk flowing around her, talk of Lothar of Wychweald and how to go about defeating him.

The dwarf promised a cage of steel and rare mined stone if Gilraehen would be so good as to strengthen it with a bit of his magic. Several men agreed with that plan, vowing to search out lads to build another army, if Gilraehen would lead it. There was talk of seeking out ancients from the school of wizards to strengthen those armies and build a force that Lothar couldn't best.

The old man with the weathered face suggested patience.

Gil's brothers vowed revenge.

The elf with the terrible beauty and the sparkling eyes cleared his throat and even Gil lifted his gaze to look at him. Mehar understood completely. She could hardly take her eyes off him.

"I think," he said, in a melodious voice that made her wonder if she croaked like a crow when she spoke, "we should consider his deeper purpose."

"And that would be?" Gil asked. "Tell me, Ainteine, what deeper purpose he has than to ruin us all?"

"You know it already, Gilraehen," Ainteine said. "Have you not seen him single out certain races and hunt them until they're gone?" He looked at Mehar and she felt as if her soul had suddenly become transparent, that he saw all that she was in one glance. "You've wed a wife of Camanaë out of love, and you also promised her safety, and that out of love as well. Perhaps destiny has had a stronger hand in it than you realize, given her dam's fate."

Alcuin leaned over to her. "Quite fond of destiny, that lot."

Mehar found herself feeling quite cold all of a sudden. "Why do you speak of my mother?" she asked Ainteine. "Did you know her?"

"We know all of Camanaë," Ainteine said, "for you are more like to us than other men."

"Are they?" Mehar asked, hardly able to believe it. "I mean, are we?"

"You are," Gil said, smiling at her gravely. "Many generations ago, Sgath of Ainneamh wed with Eulasaid of Camanaë and thus a particular line of Camanaë was begun."

"That is true, Gilraehen," Ainteine said smoothly. "And you will find yourself, as did Sgath, watching your children bear your lady's magic and searching doubly hard for ways to thwart Lothar that he does not touch them."

Mehar blinked. "What do you mean?"

She felt Gil take her hand. "What he means is that he believes most of your mother's line has fallen to Lothar's hand at one time or another."

"Your mother's was a powerful magic, one that Lothar loathes above all else, but desires likewise," Ainteine said. "Gilraehen was wise to wed you, for he alone has the strength to protect you and the children you will bear him." He looked at her gravely. "Watch yourself, Mehar of Neroche. You will need all the skills you can learn from your lord, as well as many you will only learn from yourself, to survive."

"Well, this is all fine and good," said the crusty old man, "but that hardly solves the larger problem of ridding ourselves of him for good."

Alcuin elbowed her in the ribs until she leaned his way. "Gil's mother's father, Beachan of Bargrenan. He's not much for elves or anyone else who doesn't like to get his boots muddy. We'll move on to practical matters now."

Mehar wasn't sure she wanted to move on to practical matters. She wanted to know if Ainteine had spoken to her mother, if he knew her grandmother, or her mother's grandmother, or all the other women she had never had the chance to know. She wanted everyone to pause until she'd had the answers she desired.

But it was a council of war, not a bit of a chat during supper, so she held her peace and pondered what she'd learned. And she wondered, if there truly was blood from Ainneamh running through her veins, why Ainteine could be so beautiful and she so not beautiful. Too much of her father in her, she supposed with a sigh.

She leaned her head back against her chair and waited out the discussions, which, true to Beachan's apparent schedule, moved along quite quickly; they adjourned for supper at a most reasonable hour. Mehar picked idly at her food, too overwhelmed by what she'd learned, and what she thought she'd learned, to eat.

She was almost relieved when Gil took her hand, excused them from the table, and left the hall. She was certain Alcuin was going to fill the company in on all of Gil's faults (he apparently didn't like snakes and there had been a full complement of them in Gil's annoying army the night before,) but she had little desire to stay and defend her love when she thought he might be heading for the stables and a bit of freedom.

"Is it safe?" she asked, looking at him as he reached for his horse's gear.

He stopped his movements, then looked at her. "Nay, it likely isn't. But I think I can keep us safe enough for a bit of freedom."

She didn't doubt he could. She only wished, as she saddled Fleet and led him out behind Gil's horse, that she had some kind of weapon herself.

Just in case.

But that just in case didn't seem to be waiting for them. Not that it would have mattered if it had been, given the way Gil was riding. Whether he was simply living up to his name, or whether too much talk of things he couldn't yet master had driven him to a strange mood, she couldn't have said. Fleet was the better horse, and she no poor rider, but she was hard-pressed to keep up with her love. It was a cold, crisp day, and there had been no rain in the night. The ground was bare and dry, and the chill seemed only to suit their mounts. Mehar found herself quite glad of Gil's mother's cloak, which now found a home about her own shoulders.

And then she found herself not glad at all.

Everything happened so fast, she hardly knew how to sort the events out and make sense of them.

One moment Gil was on his horse, the next he was on the ground and Fleet was lifting up to leap over him. She wheeled Fleet around and raced back only to have her horse, fearless beast that he was, pull up, and shudder.

Gil crawled to his feet, dazed.

And then, out of the shadows of the trees, came a man.

Mehar knew without being introduced that this was Lothar. He looked, oddly enough, a great deal like the Prince of Hagoth, but Mehar supposed she was beginning to lump all the horrible men she knew into one mass that wore the same sort of face Hagoth and the bounty hunter had.

Hard. Cold. Cruel.

And then, quite suddenly, not a face anymore.

What sort of creature Lothar had become, she honestly couldn't say, but he was no longer a man and just the sight of him made her want to bolt.

But Gil didn't flee. Where he had stood now hovered an enormous bird of prey, its beak outstretched, its terrible, razorlike claws reaching out to shred the beast before it.

And that was just the beginning.

Mehar lost count of the changes, of the nightmares come to life, of the curses that were hurled, the threats that were spewed, the taunts that Lothar gave and Gil ignored.

And then, just as suddenly as before, Lothar was a man again and in his hand was a sword that flashed in the sunlight. It flashed again as it struck out like a snake. Mehar watched in horror as it bit into whatever disjointed mass of creature Gil had chosen in his wrath to become; the creature bellowed and suddenly there was Gil, writhing on the ground with a sword skewering his leg.

Mehar didn't think. She dug her heels into Fleet's side, but that was unnecessary. He was a mount fit for a mighty warrior and he did what her sire had trained him to do long before she'd stolen him and bid him to be her wings. He leaped at Lothar, slashing him across the face with a hoof as he jumped.

Lothar screamed, but pulled her from the saddle by her foot just the same.

As she fell, she wove her spell of protection.

Over herself.

Over Gil.

Over Fleet.

Lothar glared at her as she lay sprawled on the ground before him. He clutched the torn side of his face and spewed forth curses at her. Mehar quailed, but her spell, the simple, blessed thing that it was, held true. Lothar took a step back.

"I will find you," he said coldly, "and when I've taken your magic, I will kill you."

Mehar didn't answer him.

He vanished, but his last words hung in the air.

Just as I did your mother.

Mehar crawled over to Gil. He was white and he'd lost a great deal of blood. She hardly dared pull the sword free, though she could only imagine the foul spells it was laced with. Her lord husband looked at her with wonder and sorrow mingled in his eyes.

"I feared that," he said quietly. "About your mother."

"How... how did he..."

Gil shook his head. "I don't know. She may have kept him from Angesand so thoroughly that he resorted to having some simple soul poison her." He grasped her hand. "All I know is she protected you. As will I."

She clutched his bloody hand with both hers. "I need a sword, Gil. Even if your hand was whole, even when it *is* whole, I'll need some way to guard your back. To guard my own if you're guarding our children. I could weave things into it."

He looked at her quietly for a moment or two, then nodded. "As you will, love. But you'll use none of this metal here. Can you pull that accursed thing free?"

"You'll bleed."

"Better that than have his magic crawling up my leg as it is presently."

"But Gil, how will I—"

Epilogue

Harold blinked, then realized his father had stopped reading. He was whispering behind his hand to one of the men in his merchantry business. Then the man departed and his father stood.

"Wait," Harold said, sitting up suddenly, "you can't stop there. What happened? Did she pull the sword out of his leg? Did Gilraehen survive? And what about her sword? The magical sword she made? The Sword of Angesand?" Harold gave his father his most potent look of pleading. "Father, you cannot leave me at this point. Finish before you leave, I beg you."

His sire hesitated, then sat back down. "Very well," he said, "I will humor you. Briefly. Though you've heard this tale a hundred times at least."

"Once more?" Harold asked hopefully.

His father sighed, but it was without irritation. "Once more," he agreed, taking up the book again. "It says here that Gilraehen and Mehar managed to get themselves atop Fleet and let him carry them back to the ruined palace, with Gil's horse following, where Cook nourished them with all useful herbs and fine stews. Then our goodly Queen Mehar—"

"The Bold," Harold put in reverently.

"Aye," his father said with a grave smile, "our goodly Queen Mehar the Bold found herself invited to the dwarf-king's palace over the mountains where she descended into the bowels of his keep and there forged her blade, weaving into it the most powerful of her mother's spells."

"Right away, or did she have to practice sword-making?" Reynauld asked. "It is, as you might not know, Father, a rather complicated business."

Harold watched their sire look at his eldest son over the top of the book. "It says that she did take a goodly bit of time at the task, son. And Ingle, the steelsmith, did take an especial interest in training her in the art, for by then Gilraehen and Mehar had searched all the pages of Elfine's book and discovered many potent spells of defense and protection which Ingle found much to his liking—"

"And what of the bride price?" Imogen interrupted impatiently. "And the price on her head? Did the king pay both?"

"He would have—" their sire began.

"And likely still would be—" interjected their mother.

"But," their father said with a smile thrown his wife's way, "the price on Mehar's head was satisfied because the dastardly Prince of Hagoth was persuaded to take another of Angesand's daughters to wife."

"How horrible!" Imogen exclaimed.

"Aye, well, Hagoth wed Sophronia of Angesand, beat her once, then found himself encountering a piece of meat too large for his throat at table two days later—and there is some question as to whether or not Sophronia was cutting his meat that day, though it doesn't say here—and died, unmourned. Sophronia took over his affairs, corralled his children, and wed herself a man quite content to let her manage him, so perhaps it wasn't so horrible after all."

"But what of the bride price?" Harold persisted. "The king paid a goodly price for Queen Mehar, didn't he? It seems as if he should have, she being such a capital fellow and all."

"Never fear, son," their father said, "it says here that a premium price was paid. The king gave our good Lord of Angesand a queenly amount of his gold, a pair of the finest brood mares left him, then laid an enchantment of excellence on Angesand's stables—an enchantment, I might add, that took nigh onto two weeks to do properly."

"Still in force, I'd say," Reynauld said pragmatically. "Passing good steeds, those beasts from Angesand. Fleet of foot and fearless in battle. Strong. Courageous. Wouldn't mind having one myself."

At this point, he looked at his father expectantly.

"I'll think on it," his father promised. "Those horses of Angesand's come dear." He looked at Harold. "Any further questions, my lad?"

"What was Queen Mehar's dowry?"

His father smiled. "Why, Fleet, of course."

"And what happened to Lothar?"

His father seemed to choose his words carefully. "He was wounded, but not mentally. He is Yngerame of Wychweald's son, after all, and because of that has untold years to count before his tally is full. He could live on endlessly."

"But you don't think so," Harold said. He'd overheard—very well, he'd eavesdropped, but how else was a lad to find out anything interesting in a hall where the conversations changed course so quickly each time a child appeared within earshot?—he had *overheard* his sire and his dam speculating on this very subject more than once.

His father looked at him sharply—perhaps he hadn't been careful enough—then sighed. "I think," he said slowly, "that Lothar will continue until he is slain. His evil is strong and he feeds on the fear he inspires in those around him. It is an endless supply of energy to him. How he will meet his end, in the end, I cannot say."

"And his sons?" Reynauld asked, looking, for once, more concerned about affairs of the realm than he was in obtaining the horse of his dreams.

"I don't think they match him in power," their father said quietly.

"But I thought Lothar was a faery tale," Imogen said in a low, quavering voice. "One you made up to frighten us when we asked for that kind of thing. I didn't think he was real."

Their father closed the book and smiled easily at her. "'Tis perhaps just that, my love. After all, few claim to have seen him. Maybe he was just a simple man who lived and died long ago —"

There was a knock, then a servant came in, leaned down, and whispered into their sire's ear. Their father excused himself quickly and went out.

"More tradespeople?" Imogen asked hopefully, her face alight with the expression Harold immediately recognized as enthusiasm over the possibility of more fabric. She even shot him a look, assessing no doubt his current state of grubbiness and how that might affect her plans.

"Mother, must I go into the merchant business?" Reynauld asked, kneeling over his battlefield. "I would so much prefer to be a warrior. On one of Angesand's finest war horses," he added casually.

"Merchantry is an honorable profession," his mother said placidly.

"It seems a tiresome business," Reynauld said. "Messengers arriving at all hours, having to closet yourself with them at all hours, endless discussions, endless bolts of cloth. You would think," he added, "that father would have chosen a more likely spot for his house, wouldn't you? Nearer the Crossroads, perhaps in the duchy of Curach, somewhere other than so far north that our most frequent arrivals are snow and ice and the only reason we have green, tender leafy things to eat is because I stoke the fires each day in that accursed glass house to keep them warm!"

And then, apparently fearing he'd said too much, he shot his mother an apologetic look, rose, then trotted off, to no doubt stoke more fires.

Imogen rose as well, with the excuse of needing to go examine her supply of red silk and see if it was sufficient. Harold watched them go, then watched his mother thoughtfully for some time. The Book of Neroche lay on a heavy, richly carved table next to her chair. He glanced at it, then back at his mother's scarred hands. Some of the scars were round, silvery circles of uneven shape, as if she'd been burned by stray sparks.

He blinked, feeling a great mist begin to clear from his mind.

Burns. Stray sparks. Stray sparks from a *smithy* perhaps?

He looked at the rest of his mother. Her hair was dark, piled on top of her head in what at the start of day was a quite restrained bun. By evening, though, it always looked as it did this evening: riotously curly and relentlessly falling off the top of her head to cascade down past her shoulders.

He thought about her killing that spider.

He wondered why indeed it was that they lived so far in the north. Why men came to see his sire at all hours. Why his sire was gone for long periods of time without a better explanation than he'd been off looking at silks.

Something he seemed to have no affinity for when he was home, truth be told.

Harold pondered yet more on questions that suddenly demanded answers. Why had he never met any of his mother's kin? Why did his father command such deference from the men who came to see him? Why did his mother often sit in her weaving chamber, whispering quietly over what she wove in a tongue he could not understand?

Reynauld never thought past his pretend battles; Imogen was content with her wares, so if they asked and were given vague answers, they never questioned further. Harold suspected the days of his doing that were over.

He sat up, walked across the rug on his knees and knelt before his mother, the questions burning his mouth. His father called her *my lady,* and his mother always called his father *my lord.* Indeed, as he looked back over his memories, he couldn't remember them calling each other anything else.

At least within his earshot.

Surely there was more to them both than that.

"Who are you?" he asked.

She looked at him in surprise, but it was followed so quickly by a gentle smile that he almost believed he'd imagined her first reaction.

"I am your mother who loves you, son."

He took his mother's hand. "Where did you get these burns?"

"From a fire."

"Is your sire alive? Your dam?"

She tilted her head to one side. "You're full of questions tonight."

"Well?"

"If you'll have the answers to those, then aye and nay."

"Why have I never met them?"

"Travel is perilous."

He frowned at her. "These are not the answers I'm seeking."

"They are the safe answers, Harry."

He frowned at her, then kissed her hand and rose.

"Where do you go, son?"

He paused at the door. "Hunting, Mother."

"'Tis bedtime, my dear."

"It will be a short hunt."

She laughed softly and he left the warmth of the family's chamber. He wondered where his parents would keep secrets, if they had any, and decided upon their bedchamber. He almost toppled his great-grandsire—his father's mother's sire—over in his haste. He looked at him sharply. Was this Alesone of Neroche's father? He knew the king's genealogy well; it was required learning from his tutor. He'd never dreamed it might apply to him. He returned his attention to the man before him.

"Who are you?" Harold demanded.

"Who do you think I am?" his great-grandsire asked with a look about him that said he'd been long anticipating the question and had wondered why it had been so long in coming.

"I think you are Beachan of Bargrenan," Harold answered.

His great-grandsire laughed. "Sharp-eyed hawk," he said affectionately, pinching Harold's cheek. "Wondered when it would come to him," he said as he walked away.

"That's no answer!" Harold bellowed after him.

Beachan of Bargrenan only held up his hand in a wave, then continued on without turning back.

Harold pressed on. He threw open the door to his parents' bedchamber. It was, he had to admit upon new observation, quite a luxurious chamber. Thick carpets were laid tidily upon the floor, and the walls were covered by equally opulent tapestries.

Things from his father's trades?

Harold suspected not. These were far and above anything he'd ever seen come in the back of a tradesman's cart.

"If I were the Sword of Angesand," he muttered, "where would I hide myself?" He looked around him, then his eyes fell upon the headboard of the bed. He walked swiftly to it and ran his fingers over the intricate carvings. Aye, they were fashioned most suspiciously in the shape of a blade, especially that long bit there covered with trailing vines. And did not that crossed piece of wood look a good deal like a sword hilt?

He contemplated for a moment how he might liberate a blade from such a covering. Something sharp to dig with, aye, that would suit. He looked about him and scowled. If someone had just lit those candles on the candelabra near his dam's night table, he might have…

He might have been able to see.

Which he did now, in spite of those unlit candles, candles resting on a long, silver stand that was, oddly enough, sword height.

If you were a woman, that was.

Harold wondered why he hadn't seen it before. Indeed, it was as if a veil of un-noticing had been pulled off his eyes and now, for the first time in eight long years, he saw clearly.

There, in plain sight, driven into a round base of black granite, was a sword. A sword with a tracery of leaves and flowers—things Queen Mehar loved—flowers that looked a great bloody bit like his mother's favorite tapestry that hung in his favorite cozy chamber, truth be told. The hilt was a simple cross, adorned with more trailing, blossoming vines where they didn't interfere with the holding of the weapon. The hilt now wore a humble tray of polished stone on which sat a handful of candles.

The Sword of Angesand.

Harold turned and leaped upon the bed with all the enthusiasm of Murcach of Dalbyford's finest hunting hounds and pressed and prodded and poked at the headboard with the candle snuffer he'd found near the candles until—to his great astonishment—part of the wood fell down and hung there by hinges. And what should be behind that wood—that sword-shaped wood—but a sword with a great, blinding blue stone embedded in its hilt.

The Sword of Neroche.

Resting above his father's pillow, of all places.

He put his hand out to touch it.

"The blade is sharp."

He squeaked in fright and whipped around to see his mother standing at the foot of the bed, hidden just a bit by the bed curtains. Harold peered around the fabric. By Tappit of Croxteth's crooked nose, had he never marked how queenly his mother looked? He found himself quite suddenly quite unable to form words—a rather alarming turn of events, to be sure.

His mother, Mehar of Angesand, Queen of Neroche.

She walked around the end of the bed, came to its head, and leaned past Harold to lift the wooden façade back up. It closed back over the sword with a firm *click*. Then his mother looked at him and smiled.

"So, my son," she said gently, "your sight has cleared."

He babbled. He stammered. He ceased his attempts at speech and merely stared at her in wonder. Then, he felt his eyes narrowing. "Why didn't you tell us?" he demanded. "Tell *me*, of all people."

She reached out and smoothed his hair out of his eyes. "My young Harry, my trusted confidant, I didn't tell you because I needed to protect you as long as I could."

"Protect me from what?" he demanded.

She gave him the look she was wont to give when he'd asked a question for which she just recently provided the answer. "Were you not listening this evening?" she asked quietly. "Did you not hear whom it is we fight—"

She stopped at the sound of footsteps outside the door. She put her finger to her lips and pointed to the shadows near the fireplace. Harold bolted across the room and hid himself behind a tapestry.

"Mehar? Ah, love, there you are."

Harold nodded in satisfaction at the sound of *that* name. So, he was right after all.

And then the full truth of it struck him with full force. He peered around the tapestry and stared at none other than Gilraehen the Fey, King of Neroche, son of Alexandir, grandson of Iamys, great-grandson of Symon, and great-great-grandson of Yngerame of Wychweald, who was the most powerful mage of all. Gilraehen.

His father.

"Alcuin says that he's seen nothing on the roads tonight—"

Then he paused and looked directly at Harold who was merely peeping out from behind the tapestry and was certain he'd been hidden well enough. He gulped.

His father didn't move. He merely stared at Harold in silence.

Harold leaped forward and threw himself to his knees before his father.

"My liege," he said, clasping his hands in front of him. "My king. Command me."

His sire regarded him with a quite noticeable lack of expression.

"Your liege? Your king? What prompts you to offer me such obeisance, my son?"

"I saw both swords," Harold admitted.

His father looked at him for another moment or two in silence, then sighed deeply and cast his wife a look. "I suppose he had to see eventually. I'm only surprised Imogen hasn't been asking questions. Did you not see her the other day, snatching looks at the spell book of Wexham?"

"Aye," Mehar said with a laugh. "The next thing we know, she'll be turning Reynauld into a toad as payment for his chopping up her dolls for use as artillery bits."

Harold could hardly believe his ears. "Imogen? She possesses *magic?*"

His mother looked at him. "She is my daughter, Harry. I daresay that you might be a Camanaë exception yourself. Your sight has cleared quite early and it was no weak spell we cast over this palace of Tor Neroche."

Tor Neroche. *Neroche of the mountains.* Harold shook his head. Why had he never seen it before? Why had he never questioned his mother more fully about her past, or questioned his sire more fully about his? And to think he himself might possess magic. That he could believe, but the thought of anyone else in his family claiming the like, especially his sister, was too much for even him. He looked at his mother.

"But Imogen," he protested. "She's just so... so..."

His father cast him a mild look of warning and Harold turned away from his thoughts of disbelief that his sister could do anything more complicated than find ways to match purple with red and make it look appealing before he borrowed trouble. He smiled weakly at his father and found a wry smile greeting him in return.

"When did you intend to tell us?" Harold asked. If his father was looking that accommodating, he might get in a few questions whilst he could. "And won't Reynauld be surprised! An Angesand steed will surely be his!"

Gilraehen laughed as he knelt down on one knee and looked at his youngest son. "Aye, that is possible, though if he thought about it hard enough, he would realize that the ancient, hoary-haired steed he tends so carefully in that unassuming stall is none other than Fleet, Queen Mehar's winged steed."

Harold could hardly believe his ears. "Fleet?" he squeaked. "That is *Fleet?*"

"Who has sired many, many fine horses that you have watched your mother ride more than once. Perhaps you haven't marked her skill."

Harold gave that some thought. He'd been generally more concerned about the bug life crawling about in the mud than his mother's skill with beasts, though he had to admit upon further reflection, that she was a capital horsewoman. He nodded at his mother, then turned back to his sire for further answers.

"When did you intend to tell me all this?" he asked again.

Gilraehen the Fey laughed and ruffled Harold's hair affectionately with a hand that was scarred—Harold could see that now—but whole.

"You *did* intend to tell me, didn't you?" Harold pressed.

"Aye," Gilraehen said, "we would have. When it was necessary. When we were prepared to wage war. When we thought Lothar could be taken."

Harold rubbed his hands together expectantly. "Well, what do we do now? What is our plan?"

Gilraehen shot Mehar a look that Harold considered far fuller of amusement than the situation warranted, but he was getting answers to his questions and he was privy to the king's counsels, so he wasn't going to take his sire to task when there were still answers to be had. He waited patiently for further enlightenment.

"How do you feel, Harold my lad, about an adventure?"

Could life improve? Harold almost leapt with joy. "An adventure?" he asked rapturously.

"Aye, my son, an adventure. But," he added seriously, "it will not be an adventure for lads with no stomach for danger. It will require courage, sacrifice, loyalty to the highest degree. And a willingness to pay whatever price is necessary to ensure victory. And even then, we cannot be assured of victory during the course of our battle. The war will be long, for the enemy is cunning and has nothing to live for save his own misery. We may fight, only to leave the ending of the war to others."

"If it means I can fight with you, Father, then the ending does not matter."

"Then put your hands in mine, son, and pledge me your fealty. And then, I suppose, we must see to fashioning you a sword. Perhaps you might ask your mother. She's quite skilled at that sort of thing."

I t was quite a bit later that Harold went to bed. His brother was already asleep, snoring as he lay on his back, sleeping the sleep of the uninformed. Harold tried not to feel superior as he sought his own bed, but he failed completely.

He had pledged fealty to Gilraehen the Fey, King of Neroche.

He had discussed the making of a sword with Mehar the Queen, his very own mother and sword-maker extraordinaire.

His head was full of visions of glory, danger, mighty deeds that would be sung of for generations to come. And he, Harold of Neroche, son of the king, would be involved in all of them.

And if that wasn't an adventure of the first order, he didn't know what was.

A Whisper of Spring

Prologue

She woke to blackness.

It took her several moments to decide if her eyes were open or not. Once she was quite certain she was awake, realization dawned—the realization that she was lying on a cold floor, without benefit of bed, fire, or even the meanest of quilts to shield her from the chill.

She paused, disoriented and confused. Was she dreaming? She supposed she might be, but this was a dream she had little liking for.

She very carefully closed her eyes and sank back into the darkness. She struggled to make herself smell air that was cool and fragrant. She listened for the crackle of the fire in her hearth and the faint sound of wind moving through bare winter branches.

She waited.

In time, she had to admit that the only sound she could hear was her own harsh, uneven breathing. The air smelled not of roses, but of something foul, and the darkness did not abate, not even when she could no longer pretend to sleep.

She shivered.

At length, the room lightened, though not overmuch. She could see but a sliver of gray sky from the slit of a window set deep into a casement across the chamber from her. She sat up and pulled her sleeping gown over her knees, then hugged her knees to her chest in a futile attempt to warm herself and stared in disbelief at her surroundings.

Gone was the riot of color that surrounded her in her own chamber, color that spread outside her window as far as the eye could see. Gone was the large bed with piles of beautiful quilts and fine blankets knitted of the softest cashmere. Gone was the magnificently carved furniture, the finely wrought tapestries, the plush rugs of muted hues and exquisite softness beneath her feet. Gone was the smell of rich earth, clean rain, and perfumed blossoms.

In its place was the smell of evil.

What, by all that was wondrous, had befallen her?

When she had the courage, she looked about herself. She was in a stone chamber. It was small and without any furnishings at all, not even a worn cushion for her head or a scrap of quilt with which to make a poor bed. The stone was gray, a dark, unrelenting gray that was not relieved by even the stingy bit of daylight that struggled in through the window slit.

After a time, she noticed a doorway across from her. She scrambled to her feet and ran across to it, jerking it open.

It was a privy.

A pity the hole there was so small. Had it been larger, she would have crawled through it, no matter where it led. She shut the door slowly, then leaned her forehead against it, wondering what she would do now. The chill of the floor bit into her feet, forcing her away from the door and back into her corner. At least there, her own warmth had made some minute change in temperature. She resumed her crouch and did her best to still the fear that threatened to choke her.

Apparently, she succeeded, and so thoroughly that it took her several minutes to realize she was no longer alone in her prison. A man was leaning against the wall to her right, watching her.

She forced herself to her feet and wrapped her arms around herself, more for the comfort of that embrace than any protection it might have offered.

The man pushed away from the wall and made her a low bow.

She recoiled. She couldn't help herself. There was something quite fraudulent about that appearance of deference. The back of her head touched the wall and she flinched as she reached up to find a lump there.

Memory flooded back. She'd been tending her fire for the final time before bed when a shadow had fallen across her. She remembered a sharp pain, then nothing more. Had this been the man who had dared enter her chambers? Obviously so, else she wouldn't find herself captive in his hall. Perhaps he had also dared attack her. Clearly he knew nothing about her or he never would have.

"You struck me," she said disapprovingly.

"Aye," he replied simply, without remorse.

She frowned. "No one has dared strike me before."

"I daresay they haven't."

She looked at him, quite unable to believe he was so bold. "Have you no idea who I am?"

"Aye," he said. "You are Iolaire, daughter of the High King of Ainneamh."

"You know, yet you dared steal me?" she asked, incredulous.

He only shrugged, apparently unrepentant.

"Have you no idea what my father will do to you?"

He smiled, but somehow that smile did not reach his eyes. "Elves do not come after those who dare leave elven lands, do they? So, given that your father will remain comfortably and safely ensconced upon his throne, I daresay I know exactly what he will do to me."

She suppressed the urge to rub her arms. "Who are you?"

"Lothar of Wychweald."

Wychweald? She knew Yngerame, the mage king of Wychweald, but there was only good attached to his name. Did this man seek to borrow some of that reputation to burnish his own? Surely the two men were not related...

A pity she had not bothered to learn more about the kingdoms of men. She knew enough to be pleasant at supper to those rare mortals who were allowed into her land to curry her father's favor. She had been destined to wed another of her kind, so what need had she had to learn of the outside world?

She wished now that she had made the effort.

Well, whoever this man was, he was surely not her equal either in power or station. She put her shoulders back. "What do you want?" she demanded.

"You."

She blinked. "Me? Why?"

"I need a bride."

She looked at him, dumbfounded. "A bride?"

"I tried your cousin Ceana." He shrugged. "She said nay."

Iolaire swallowed past her parched throat. So that was where Ceana had gone. She'd thought her cousin had gone mad and left home for the love of a mortal. "Where is she now?"

"Dead."

She smothered a cry of horror with her hand. What kind of man...

"Think on it," he said simply. "I'll return." A doorway appeared in the rock, he left through it, then the doorway disappeared.

Iolaire rushed to it, ran her hands over it, but found nothing.

No opening.

Nothing but rock.

Nothing but her doom.

She walked back to her corner, sank down to the cold floor, and wept. Whoever he was, Lothar of Wychweald knew of what he spoke. Her people would not come for her; they would assume she had gone because she had chosen to. A part of her suspected that even if her father knew she had been abducted, he wouldn't come to search for her. The intrigues of men held no interest for him. He would, no matter the truth of it, consider her to have dabbled in those affairs at her own peril.

She was alone and without aid.

She closed her eyes and squeezed herself back into the corner as tightly as possible. Perhaps if she tried hard enough, she would wake and find it had all been a very foul dream.

But she suspected she wouldn't.

Her heart broke, and the sound of it echoed in the stillness of the chamber.

One

The fire burned brightly in the hearth, warming not only the rugs before it, but also the dogs lying upon those rugs and the man sitting in the least uncomfortable chair in what was almost a snug gathering chamber. Tapestries depicting glorious scenes of the hunt lined the stone walls and drove away yet more of the chill. The dogs dozed, their hind legs twitching now and again as they dreamed of the chase. Winter raged outside, but inside all were safe and secure, if not quite cozy, before that cheery blaze.

But as Symon of Neroche sat before the fire with a cup of ale in one hand and his other hand pressed over his eyes, he found that even a pleasant fire could not drive away the chill of the tidings he was receiving. He rubbed his eyes, sighed, then looked at his oldest friend who was, as fate would have it, also his chief advisor and captain of his guard.

"Say that again," Symon instructed. "But slowly. I didn't sleep well last night."

"Bad beds," Hamil said promptly. "This is, as you may or may not remember, your father's hunting lodge. There is a decided lack of creature comforts here."

"We have a roof, a fire and food," Symon replied. "It will have to suffice us at present. Now, please give me the tidings again."

Hamil blew out a gusty breath of impatience. "Again, there are still reports of attacks from the north, rumors of things coming across the border at night —"

"What sorts of things?" Symon interrupted, but he didn't need to ask the question; he already knew the answer. He listened to Hamil recount the tidings, but he'd already heard the scouting reports filled with tales of creatures that had once been men but now were not, rumors of abductions of innocent crofters, tales of narrow escapes from horrors normally confined to nightmares, glimpses of a castle near the sea that bled darkness across the land it controlled, darkness that had begun to seep southward across Neroche's northern border.

Nay, Symon was not sleeping well at all.

"Will you hear more?" Hamil asked.

Symon shook his head. "I've heard enough, thank you." He spared an unkind thought for his father. It was that old fox's fault that Symon was freezing in a drafty hunting lodge, unable to wear the crown of Neroche—which fit so poorly that Symon's cook was using it for a pastry mold—and facing an unrelenting onslaught from the north, an onslaught that his father had suddenly tired of a year ago.

Damn him anyway.

Symon sighed heavily. "Is there anything else? Something I can solve easily?"

"Your father sent word," Hamil offered. "He wishes to know how your search for a bride proceeds."

Symon rubbed his forehead with a bit more vigor. "I imagine he does."

"He has given up on sending you suggestions. Instead, your mother sent along a list. I have it here"—he patted his breast protectively—"should you care to have a look at it."

"I wouldn't."

"She claims it will inspire you," Hamil said, as if he hadn't heard Symon's answer. "And if you don't mind me pointing this out to you, my unwed but quite eligible friend, you have no roster of potential brides loitering upon your person."

Symon now used two hands to rub his face.

"Of course," Hamil continued, "I can make you a copy of your mother's suggestions for your own study, if you like, whilst I retain the original in case you strike through a name or two, then regret your haste later —"

The door burst open. Guards who had been standing silently in the shadows leapt forward, then stopped still. Hamil was up with his sword drawn, then he froze as well. Symon found himself on his feet along with the rest, without really knowing how he'd gotten there. He stared at the intruder, supposing idly that he might be allowed a bit of surprise. It wasn't every day that an elf deigned to visit a mortal's dwelling. But the elf in question seemed unfazed by his break with tradition. He merely walked across the small hall calmly, as if it were no great thing to be who he was, where he was.

Symon cleared his throat. "Ehrne of Ainneamh, son of Proìseil the Proud," he managed, scrambling to dredge up a few polite phrases in his somewhat unused elvish. "You grace my hall with your presence."

"I congratulate you on that honor," Ehrne replied easily in his own tongue.

"Foolish is the man who does not realize when such an honor is bestowed upon him."

"And wise is the king who recognizes when he is being so honored. Wise in spite of his youth and inexperience with his crown," he added.

Symon suppressed a sigh. He was five and thirty, old enough to manage the affairs of one small kingdom. Never mind that Neroche was a vast land surrounding several smaller of the Nine Kingdoms. Never mind that he'd spent so much of his time over the past year trying to keep the evil from the north at bay that he hadn't seen a fraction of that kingdom. Never mind that instead of giving him decent warning, his father had, a year earlier, plopped that ill-fitting crown on his head one night at supper and bid him pack his bags the next morning and be about his next adventure. He would rule well enough, if he could just have the peace to do it in.

Symon gestured with his most regal gesture towards Hamil's chair. "Will you take your ease?"

Hamil, mercifully, abandoned his chair without comment. He fetched a stool from the hearth and sat down upon it, still silent and slack-jawed.

Symon waited until Ehrne had seated himself with a grace that belied the great distance he'd come and, by the telling condition of his clothes, the haste in which he'd traveled it, before he slowly took his seat. Why in the world a prince of Ainneamh would find himself in a snow-bound hunting lodge leagues from his own comfortable home—

"I came to seek your aid."

Symon stared at him, dumbfounded. "I beg your pardon?"

"You have magic, I assume, being the son of a mage king."

"Aye, well, I suppose I do."

Ehrne looked at him appraisingly. "Let us be about discussing the depth and breadth of it before I decide if I've chosen amiss—"

"Use the common tongue!" Hamil exclaimed suddenly. He looked at Symon crossly. "You know I cannot decipher that elvish babbling."

Symon supposed Hamil deserved the long look Ehrne gave him, but so be it. Even if Hamil could speak the language of Ainneamh as well as Symon himself could, there was safety in having a relative stranger think him incapable of understanding his tongue. It might prove useful in the future.

"Your magic," Ehrne repeated, turning his attention back to Symon. "I would know—"

"And I would know what your business if first," Symon said as politely as he could. "Lest there be no need for a discussion of whatever paltry skills I might possess."

Ehrne paused only for a moment before he shrugged. "That is fair enough, I suppose. I am here because I was banished."

Symon blinked in surprise. "You were what?"

"I was banished. By my father, in case you were wondering."

That answered one question, but raised several more. "Why?"

"I was accused of trying to kill the queen."

"The queen," Symon said slowly. "Morag."

"Aye."

"Morag, your mother."

"Aye there, too." Ehrne looked about him purposefully, but apparently fruitlessly.

Symon handed him the half-full cup of ale he held in his own hands. Ehrne drained it, then dragged his sleeve across his mouth.

"Drinkable. Barely."

"We do our best," Hamil said stiffly from his corner.

Ehrne looked at him, or through him rather, then turned back to Symon. Symon motioned for his page to refill the prince's cup, then accepted another for himself.

He sipped slowly while his guest quenched his thirst with barely drinkable ale and while he waited, he considered. This was a remarkable visit, no matter the true reason. It wasn't every day a man entertained an elf of Prince Ehrne's pedigree and station.

Though, it wasn't that Symon hadn't treated with elves before. He had. He'd become acquainted with their fine tastes, their diplomatic speech, their painful beauty—on those rare occasions when they had come to make visits of state to his father. He had also been to Ainneamh—and for longer than most men could claim.

Long enough to look on things he never should have seen, to be burned by a beauty so painful, even the memory of it made him want to draw his hand over his eyes.

A beauty whose brother had apparently finally drunk enough to find his voice.

Ehrne looked about him as if he sought a distraction. "We heard that your father had divided his lands and made you king over the greatest part of them. Passing foul of him to leave you this hovel as your palace."

"He thought it would do me good to begin my reign humbly."

Ehrne snorted. "It would do you good to build something more suitable, lest important guests such as myself find themselves slighted."

"I'll see to it—right after we've discussed your business," Symon said. "Give me all the particulars, if you will. You say your father banished you, but I don't understand why there was no one there to protest your innocence."

"That was a bit hard to find, given that I'm quite guilty."

Symon was actually grateful for the magnitude of Hamil's gasp, for it quite handily covered his own. He tried to look as diplomatically unsurprised as possible. "Well," he said, finally. "I assume you had good reason for it." He paused. "Did you?"

Ehrne shrugged. "I suppose it depends on your perspective. I thought I had reason. You see, my mother betrayed an elf to a black mage."

Well, that would do it. "Not many of those about," Symon said, holding out his cup to his page for another filling. "Black mages, that is, not elves."

"Very few indeed," Ehrne agreed.

So few that Symon could bring all three of them to mind without effort. "So why come to me? Especially considering—"

"The fact that we hold wizards, their get, and mage kings in the same high regard as we hold rats, dwarves, and ill-dressed brigands?"

Symon smiled. "Something like that."

"The elf was kidnapped by Lothar of Wychweald."

"Ah," Symon said, somehow quite unsurprised. Aye, there was one of the three.

"And given that Lothar of Wychweald is your brother, I thought perhaps you might have an idea how to kill him."

Symon pursed his lips, even less surprised, if possible, than before. Why had he not seen this coming? "You attempted matricide and look where it got you. Is fratricide any less grievous?"

"You're the king. You'll pardon yourself."

"And you're Proìseil's heir; that didn't serve you any." Symon expected no reply and he didn't get one. "Well, who did Lothar steal?"

"My sister Iolaire."

Symon heard a cup hit the stone floor. There was also a splat, as if a goodly amount of ale had abruptly left that cup. He looked down and realized that it had been his cup to deposit its contents on his boots and the floor both.

"Do you know her?" Ehrne asked mildly.

Symon looked up. Ehrne was watching him with clear, untroubled eyes, waiting. Symon took a deep breath. "You know damned well I do."

Well, if one could call gazing at the radiant beauty of the moon whilst knowing you would never touch it, knowing. Hadn't Ehrne watched Symon watch Iolaire from across Proìseil's glittering hall? Symon had been one of the few of those perennially unpopular wizards' get to be allowed, however reluctantly it might have been, inside Proìseil's hallowed halls. Obviously being Yngerame of Wychweald's son had its advantages.

Of course, not advantage enough to do aught but look on Proìseil's fairest daughter and wish he might manage to exchange the odd courtly pleasantry—not that the princess would have wanted to exchange anything else, especially rings of betrothal or passionate kisses in her father's ever-blooming gardens.

Elves and mages did not wed. It was just one of those things that was as accepted as the sun rising in the east or the seasons changing from year to year. Then again, in that blessed land of Ainneamh seasons didn't change all that much, so perhaps there were other things that might not be as true as he'd been led to believe.

He closed his eyes briefly and brought to mind the vision of a slender young woman dressed in a gown of hues that seemed to shift as she did. But what didn't change was the sheet of darkness of her hair falling down her back and the vivid blue of her eyes. Aye, he'd been close enough to see that much, and to smell the sweet scent of her perfume as she passed by him, and to take note of the flawless perfection of her skin. If there were grace, beauty, or goodness to be found anywhere in any of the Nine Kingdoms, it was in Ainneamh, where Iolaire the Fair walked over green grass that never faded to brown—

Aye, he knew her.

He also knew that he could never have her.

"Will you help me?"

Symon came back to himself in time to hear the question. "Aye," he said, without hesitation.

"What?" Hamil bellowed. "Have you gone mad?"

Quite likely, Symon thought to himself. He listened to Hamil make increasingly loud and quite reasonable arguments as to why the entire adventure was doomed from the start, not the least of which was that even should they manage to free Iolaire from Lothar's hall, Symon could expect no more than a nod in thanks—if that. Was that worth putting his own life and kingdom at risk? He was unwed; he had no heir. Should he die, who would inherit his lands? His elder brother, the black mage in question, would have gladly and quite legally taken the title of King of Neroche, but what would have been left of his lands after a single season?

Darkness, death, destruction.

"Dangerous," Hamil was saying. "Dangerous and pointless. What you need to be doing, my liege, is following your father's advice and seeking a bride. You cannot wed with elven get and even if you did, what would it serve you? She is as banished as he is."

"My sister will wed in time," Ehrne said confidently. "Perhaps to

a wizard from the east with immense wealth and power to match."
He swept Symon's hall with a glance that spoke much of his opinion
on the place and the depths of Symon's purse.

"Do you *want* him to help you or not?" Hamil demanded. "Why
don't you go instead and pester one of those other wizards with gold
enough to raise an army to contend with Lothar?"

"He is Yngerame of Wychweald's son. One would hope that
some of the father's power became the son's upon taking his crown."
Ehrne smiled grimly at Symon. "Though Wychweald is still a powerful kingdom and Yngerame a powerful king, Neroche is larger
and you are younger."

"And I am Lothar's brother," Symon added wearily.

"Slaying your brother is easier than slaying your son. Another
reason for my appearance here and not at your father's hall."

Hamil only snorted. Perhaps he could decide on no decent re-
tort for that.

Symon sighed. "I'll go and expect nothing in return."

"Which is what you will have," Ehrne agreed. "That is assuming
you can be of any use to me. Your father is powerful, but of you I
know little—"

"I daresay you know nothing at all!" Hamil exclaimed. "My
liege not only earned the rings of mastery from all six schools of wizardry at Beinn òrain by the time he was a score, he earned the last
and final ring as well."

"I didn't know there was a seventh ring," Ehrne said, looking at
Hamil skeptically.

"There is a seventh ring, though only five of them have been
fashioned given that only five have been achieved," Hamil said im-
portantly.

"Hamil," Symon warned, trying to stave off what would no
doubt prove to be a very long retelling of a tale better left for a night
when everyone had slipped well into their cups.

Ehrne looked at Symon's hand. "I don't see any ring there."

"I think that we—" Symon began.

"It's hidden in the rye bin," Hamil supplied helpfully. "My liege tends to lose bits of his gear if they're small."

Symon rubbed his hands together purposefully. "Let us be about this—"

"Still, how will you do what needs to be done, I wonder?" Ehrne asked, doubtfully. "I've seen no performance of your skill—"

"Don't waste your strength fretting over it," Hamil said briskly. "We'll tell you of it all when we return."

"But I'm coming along," Ehrne said blankly.

"You are not," Hamil said, sounding horrified.

"But of course I am. I have my own magic."

"Aye, causing flowers to bloom and clouds to drop only as much rain as you need to keep those flowers blooming." Hamil snorted. "Look at you. You even look like a weak-stomached, flower-picking—"

Symon watched with only faint alarm as Ehrne rose and drew a sword from a previously nonexistent scabbard and made a ferocious swipe at Hamil. Hamil rose to his feet with a yawn, which would have made Symon laugh, but this was no time for levity. It was also no time to have all the decent furniture he owned carved up unnecessarily—and elf though he might have been, Ehrne was in every respect Hamil's equal. Too much longer and those two would reduce everything usable to rubble.

Symon sighed, then lifted a finger and murmured a word of command. Ehrne and Hamil's swords both went flying across the hall.

Hamil cursed and sat down.

Ehrne turned and looked at Symon with what Symon was sure had to be one of the first times in his life he'd been surprised. But the look of surprise quickly faded to satisfaction.

"I chose well, I see," he said.

"You still look like an elf," Hamil muttered.

Ehrne's stained but obviously finely made clothes disappeared and were replaced by what Symon was certain Ehrne considered ill-dressed brigand's gear.

Hamil threw up his hands and heaved himself back to his feet. "Very well, I give in. I'll go see to supplies." He looked at Symon. "When do we leave?"

"Now," Ehrne said.

Symon smiled at his captain. "Within the hour, if you please. Even elves must eat now and then."

Ehrne followed Hamil from the chamber. "I'll go with you and see to the supplies. I am no doubt the only one with the ability to see us fed well."

"I daresay that if you don't stay out of my way, the only ability you'll have will be to lie on the floor and let me use you to wipe my feet on."

Symon sighed. It was going to be a very long journey.

He wondered about the end of it. First was the question of even freeing Iolaire from his brother's castle. Perhaps it was possible. But he thought again of those first-hand accounts of what crept over Neroche's most northern borders. To think on what Lothar had done to his own people was horrifying.

But to think on what Lothar would do to an elf of Iolaire's beauty and grace?

He rose to his feet. An hour was too long to sit and wait for preparations to be made. Indeed, he rued the time he'd spent in conversation with Ehrne.

Nay, he would have nothing more than thanks from her, if that, but it would be enough.

Two

✦

Iolaire dreamed of Ainneamh.

The dream was so pleasant and so real that she smiled and stretched in her sleep. Water trickled over and down chiseled bits of polished granite from the mines of Dèan An, unearthed from deep in the elven mountains of Tòrr Dòrainn. The sounds of water softly filling the air were accompanied by heady smells from the twisting vines of jasmine and curling branches of climbing roses that framed her window. Her room was drenched in the scents of the flowers that bloomed all year round save that pair of months in the chill of winter when the earth rested and regained her strength.

The scent changed. She walked through her father's hall with the enormous hearths at each end, where a fire was lit each night to stave off the cool of the evenings. Her father was there, her brothers, her cousins, her friends, all in their finery, all eating the most delicious things her father's cooks could produce and sipping sweet wine that tasted of dew. Everything glittered, from the whisper-thin goblets hand blown by her father's most skilled glasswrights to the gowns that seem to have been spun from the gossamer wings of Ainneamh's most beautiful butterflies.

She looked about her. Her mother was gone, but that was not unusual these days. Her mother had withdrawn from them more and more often of late, as if she found their company painful. Perhaps she was grieved for the loss of her niece, Ceana. Perhaps she merely wearied of their company. Iolaire did not know and it troubled her.

But despite that niggling doubt over her mother's absence, Iolaire relished the feeling of being comfortable, safe, and surrounded by those who loved her and whom she loved. Was there a more beautiful place than Ainneamh? Was there a more luxurious and appealing hall than her father's, where the colors, sounds, and smells all blended in a perfection that was only to be found here? She drew a shawl of the finest cashmere around her shoulders and closed her eyes briefly to better savor the pleasure of it. She was certain that the bliss of her life could be no richer.

And then she saw him.

Even in her dream, she felt a tingle of something that was not dread and certainly not fear run through her. The man was not altogether mortal, but not elven-\kind either. Who he was might prove to be as much a mystery as what he was. A guest of her father's surely, else he would not have dared enter the king's innermost hall. No crown sat upon his dark hair, but he carried himself in a straight, confident way that bespoke noble breeding. He was deferential to her kin, speaking in their tongue, which was a most unusual thing for one who was not of Ainneamh, but even so, he did not abase himself...

She watched him look about the chamber as politely as good manners would allow, but with an awe she supposed she could understand well enough.

But then he turned that looking upon her.

And she watched him go still.

The same stillness came over her, leaving her feeling as if it were just they two who stood there, connected, silent and unmoving in a sea of strangers. That same feeling came over her, only this time she recognized it for what it was: a remembering. It was as if she had always known him, but only forgotten until this moment that she did.

Even eternity held its breath.

She wanted to go to him, to take his hand, to go into his arms and find herself whole. But before she could move, her brother had taken her by the arm and pulled her away. She wasted time convincing him that she was well and not consorting with mortals beneath her station, but by the time she turned back to look for the man, he was gone, lost in a sea of elves who suddenly looked all the same.

She almost wept. She looked amongst her family, but could not find him for the press of her kinfolk. After a time, she gave up and left the hall. As she walked past the mingling crowd, she thought she heard her name. She looked up quickly and saw the man again, briefly, only to have the crowd draw together before her and hide him from her view.

She didn't dare ask who he was. Her father would have wanted to know why she desired the name of a man who could not possibly interest her. Ehrne would have come undone at the thought of her looking twice at a man whose clothing was likely quite serviceable in a mortal kingdom, but made him look a rough peasant in her father's grand hall. She half wondered, now, if she would recognize him at all, or if she would pass him on a deserted road and not know it was he.

The sorrow of that was so great that she woke with tears streaming down her cheeks. And once she was awake and again facing the hard, unyielding stone of her prison, she wept for other reasons.

She would never see her home again. Even if she could free herself, she would be forever barred from it. The law was such and her father was bound to uphold it. She could break herself and her shattered heart against that law, but it would not yield.

She was alone now, without home or lover.

How she longed for both.

She leaned her bruised head gently against the wall and gave herself over to daylight dreaming. Of her home she could think no more. Her grief would be endless and thinking on it only deepened that grief.

But that man, aye, that was something she could think on idly and not have it pain her so much. Was he mage, prince, or stableboy? It had been impossible to tell, though she supposed no stableboy could have spoken her tongue and she had watched him converse with her kin. And no stableboy she'd ever encountered had possessed such a handsome face and such piercing, pale eyes. Blue or green? She could not say, and she found that it became increasingly difficult to imagine up the contours of his face. She struggled, trying to make out his features in the semi-dark of her prison.

And then the face she was seeing began to speak.

She came to herself to find Lothar of Wychweald standing on the other side of the stone chamber, speaking to her. It took her a moment or two to drag herself from the comfort of her dreaming and understand him. She frowned.

"I beg your pardon?" she said.

His look was mild, but she was no fool. And only a fool would have missed the malice behind that pleasant expression.

"I asked you if you had decided upon an answer."

Somehow, sitting there hugging her knees and pressing herself back into a corner was far too powerless a position to be in. She scrambled to her feet. "I am unsure of the question."

His snort of laughter was humorless. "I asked you if you were ready to leave the chamber."

She studied him, wondering what it would mean if she said aye. "If I say I am, to what have I agreed?"

"I think you might know," he said.

She wrapped her arms around herself, somewhat alarmed by how chilled her flesh was. "You cannot keep me locked in here forever."

He only looked at her placidly, without comment.

"Is that how you must convince me?" she demanded, her teeth

beginning to chatter. "By starving me? By denying me even the most paltry of comforts?"

He shrugged. "I hope to inspire you to come willingly." He looked at her without the slightest bit of interest or affection. "I can force you, but I imagine you wouldn't care for that."

She would have answered, but found that her mouth was suddenly too dry with panic for sound.

And she feared greatly the sound she would make if she began to give voice to her fear.

Lothar pushed away from the wall, much as he had done the first time. He spoke no word, but suddenly a doorway appeared and a door swung open.

He left, silently.

Once he was gone, Iolaire stumbled across the chamber. She ran her hands fruitlessly over the place where the doorway had been. The magic there was strong, stronger than she was accustomed to. Then again, her magic was given to more noble purposes than locking unwilling prisoners in cold, comfortless cells of stone.

She sighed deeply, then turned and went to the window. It was far too small for her to crawl through; indeed, she could scarce shove her hand through the narrow, vertical shaft that afforded her all the light her chamber possessed. She tore off the hem of her nightgown and held it bunched in her hand. Rain fell softly, slowly, but eventually long enough that the cloth was wet and she managed to draw off a small bit of moisture.

It tasted far better than anything she had ever savored at her father's table.

She spent the better part of that day trying with only scant success to ease her thirst. When evening fell and the misting rain ceased, she retreated to her corner where the draft was less, drew into the smallest folding possible of herself, and gave thought to her future.

She could wed with Lothar, she supposed. It might at least gain her an exit from her prison. She might be able to flee at some point in the future, when she had the means of escape and hope of a refuge.

But if she wed with him, she would no doubt bear him children. Unbidden, came the vision of a small, fair-skinned maid child with curling hair and soft blue eyes. Iolaire fancied that if she'd had the light for seeing, she could have looked down in her arms and seen that wee girl snuggled there, sleeping peacefully with her hands clasped together and her face turned upward, untroubled by unpleasant dreams.

Iolaire shuddered. How could she doom that child—and the rest of the world—to the specter of Lothar's manifest evil coupled with her magic?

If she had any magic left.

She gave thought to that. She had been born with magic in her blood; all elves were so blessed. At least they were as long as they remained within the borders of their land. There, spells fell over everyone and everything as effortlessly as sunlight sparkling and glistening through dew-laden trees. Elves walked through those spells, over them, under them, making the magic a part of themselves as they passed. And Ainneamh was the source of it all.

Or so she had been led to believe.

Now, though, she wondered. Losing that magic was part of what made the specter of banishment so awful. But what if the magic was in her and of her, in spite of where she dwelt?

She tried to draw magic from the stones beneath her feet, from the air, from the gray light that came in the window. In Ainneamh the magic so drawn would have shimmered in her hands and effortlessly become what she required. Here she only drew evil to her. She gasped and ceased immediately. She would have no part of this place or its power.

Though that she had even managed to gather some of it to her was something to think on.

She allowed herself another moment or two to envision again

the sweet, pure child who had not yet rested in her arms, then forced herself to give somber thought to just what she might do.

She crossed the chamber to where she knew the door to be and ran her hands over the stone. She tried *door* and *open* in all the languages she knew, but to no avail. She cursed it with all the vile things her younger brother Artair had taught her when their tutor had been snoozing in the afternoon sunlight. That brought no better result.

But as she stood there with her hands pressed against the wall, her head bowed, tears she could not spare falling down her cheeks, she realized Lothar's spell lay over where she knew the doorway to be like a piece of cloth. She pulled back with her palms still flat against that invasive bit of magic and stared at it in surprise.

Could she unravel it?

And what would Lothar do to her if she managed it?

She decided immediately that it was best not to think on that. She would seek to undo his evil quietly and perhaps she would manage to free herself from her prison, escape out the front door, and be on her way before he was the wiser.

It did not serve her to think on what would happen to her otherwise.

Three

Symon surveyed his brother's domain and could scarce believe his eyes. Gone was the lovely castle on the edge of the sea, surrounded by fair meadows full of wildflowers. Gone too were the beautiful stretches of beach before the castle, the clutches of rocks with wild birds perching thereupon, the lovely white cliffs that provided a bastion of safety from the crashing waves.

In their places were ruin and decay.

"By Crea of Meith's knobby knees, will you look at that!" Hamil exclaimed. "He's ruined the place!"

Ruin had been Symon's own word, but he saw now that 'twas too mild a term. But hadn't he suspected as much when he thought of Lothar overrunning Neroche?

Darkness, death, destruction.

He'd wondered, over the past year since he'd been king, and for several years before that, if he were imagining Lothar's potential for evil. He'd wondered it as he had watched his elder brother whilst they grew to manhood together. Lothar's power was perhaps unmeasured, but his capacity for cruelty had been amply demonstrated over the years. Symon had also wondered, when their father had given Lothar his most beautiful bit of land but no crown as an inheritance, what would become of the magnificent castle on the sea. When he'd asked as much, his father had only looked at him in that way he had, placid and patient, and said that 'twas no longer his affair and that Lothar would have to find his own way.

Did a father know, then, when a son was a babe, that the son would go so astray?

And if so, what could he possibly do to stop it?

Ah, but such a departure from good sense and goodness. Symon shook his head. Slabs of rock from ill-conceived and poorly executed mining ventures littered the land, blackness from fire, debris and refuse covered the strand—and not a green thing remained in sight. It was as if anything within Lothar's reach that had possessed any life at all had given up.

"What does he eat?" Ehrne inquired politely.

"I wouldn't want to know," Hamil said with a grimace. "Well, my liege, what now?"

Symon looked at Ehrne. "Can you sense her?"

Ehrne stood there with a look of distaste on his visage. "The stench of evil that lingers behind in Iolaire's chamber is the same as what comes from this place." He sighed and turned to Symon. "But I have no sense of her." He paused. "In truth, I have no sense of anything living."

Hamil shifted. "I don't know about that. I have little magic of my own, but I'm well acquainted with Lothar's use of his. Are there invisible companies of his monsters lying in wait to attack upon his command?"

Symon looked, but could see nothing but what appeared before him. If the castle were covered by some sort of spell, Symon could not tell.

And he was not the lesser of his father's sons.

"I daresay he has used no magic to augment the destruction," Symon said slowly, "and I can see no souls lying in wait for us."

"How does he convince people to serve him?" Ehrne asked idly.

"He steals them," Symon said. "Or perhaps I am wrong and he draws to himself those who love his particular sort of magic." He shrugged. "I do not know and I wish to know no more of it than I must to rescue your sister. So, let us be about this business and quickly, before she must spend another night in this accursed place."

"Aye," Ehrne agreed. "But let us approach as if we were lords come for a parley." He paused and looked at Symon. "Well, I will go as a lord; you may come along as my lowly squire."

"And what of me?" Hamil demanded.

"Can you shapechange?" Ehrne asked Symon.

"Aye," Symon answered.

"Can you change that one there," Ehrne asked, pointing to Hamil, "into a jackass?"

Symon laughed in spite of himself. "I have no idea why there is such enmity between the two of you, and nay, I will not change him into the like."

"Is it that you cannot, or that you will not?" Ehrne pressed. "Does your magic extend to those kinds of things, or can you only manage the simple spells a village witch could cast?"

Hamil rolled his eyes. "Know you nothing of the rings of mastery? Any fool might win the first, or even the second, but the rest are only taken by those with an affinity for the business or strong power found running through their veins. But the last ring — "

"I can manage what needs to be done," Symon interrupted with a warning look shot Hamil's way. It wasn't as though he cared what Ehrne knew of him, but there was no sense in boasting of any skill so near to Lothar's front stoop. He looked at his men and considered. "Perhaps you lads would be safer if you went about disguised as something of the equine persuasion."

The small company of his most elite guardsmen who had accompanied him north sighed almost as one. Symon supposed they could expect no less, being his men. He looked at Hamil. "And you? Shall you be the wind?"

"Make it an ill-wind and I'll say no more."

Symon nodded. As quietly as possible, in a magical sense, he made the necessary changes to his company, then changed his own appearance. Whether or not it would fool his brother remained to be seen.

Lothar had magic, 'twas true, but he had learned it not from those who taught restraint and honor in its use, but rather from rogue wizards who had learned enough to be dangerous but hadn't managed to earn any of the rings of mastery. Nay, Lothar would wear only the first of mastery, if he wore one at all. Even so, that did not mean he had no power.

Ehrne led them down the path to the hall door in a lordly fashion. Symon followed, too busy watching the surrounding desolation for the potential of attack to worry overmuch about what Ehrne would do. If they gained the great hall, hell would be unleashed upon them no matter how pretty Ehrne's introductions were.

All, however, was quiet.

Too quiet.

Ehrne banged on the door. It was opened eventually by a stooped, misshapen old man.

"I'm here to see the lord of Rathlin. Let me pass."

He did not wait for a reply, but pushed past the old man. Symon slipped in behind him. He used Ehrne's blustering calls for service as a shield so he could be about his own business. He could not hear Iolaire, nor could he sense her. He followed Ehrne into the middle of the hall near the fire pit, mentally searching frantically through passageways that were cob wedded by rotting, though dishearteningly strong magic.

And still no trace of her.

Ehrne's calls for ale grew stronger.

"Looking for someone?" cackled the old man near Symon's ear.

"I'm but the servant," Symon muttered, brushing him away.

"The hell you are."

Symon turned, realizing too late that his brother was lord and doorman both—and perilously good at hiding his identity. Before

Symon could lift a finger or spew out a spell of his own, Lothar had cast a net of his own magic.

Symon watched it fall.

I olaire selected a thread of magic that looked as if it might be weak enough for her to break. It had taken her most of the night to manage to find even that. Of course, she had been clumsy with fear, certain that Lothar would surprise her with another visit as she was about her work.

But now, as the chamber had lightened enough to signal full daylight, she had found what she sought. She unraveled a bit more on either side of that weakened thread, and then with a great rending sound that she feared would shake the castle to its foundations, she tore the spell asunder.

The door was revealed.

S ymon could have sworn the castle rocked on its foundations. The sound of rending was nothing short of deafening. Lothar, startled, turned.

And by the time he turned back, it was too late. Perhaps he was powerful. Perhaps he was determined. But Symon fought for a more noble purpose. It was the smallest of advantages, but perhaps it would be enough.

He countered Lothar's spells one by one. They were unpleasant spells, ones full of evil portents Symon had never before considered. It took all his wits to fight them off while doing his best to lay his own snares about his brother.

"Do you need aid?" Ehrne asked from beside him. "Shall I put the kettle on? Toss herbs onto the fire? Brew up a potion or two?"

"Shut up," Symon said, through gritted teeth. "Be about our other business."

"And what is that?" Lothar said, sounding equally taxed. "The rescuing of an elven princess? You needn't bother. She's dead already."

Symon gasped in surprise, then staggered under the renewed onslaught of Lothar's spells. He would have bid Ehrne make a search, but he didn't have the breath for any speaking.

And then Lothar smiled and began the words of essence changing. Symon was torn between a desire to point out to his brother where he was doing it wrong and the horror of realizing that his brother was trying to weave such a spell around him. It took all his strength to counter the spell, to fight it off with his own magic.

He felt himself, after what seemed like hours, begin to weaken.

The ground beneath him began to slip.

And slip a bit more.

As eternity passed, he began to wonder if he would manage to best his brother after all.

Out of the corner of his eye, he saw another old man enter the hall. Damnation, was he to be plagued by these geriatric pretenders until the end?

He realized, perhaps the instant before his brother did, that this old fool was not quite what he seemed either. If Symon had had the strength, he would have sighed in relief, no matter how unkingly it might have made him look.

Yngerame of Wychweald had arrived and he did not look pleased.

Four

Iolaire crept toward the stairs, her bare feet crunching things she didn't stop to identify. She was free of her prison and on her way to being free of the castle. There was noise coming from the stairwell before her, as if there were a great ruckus happening below in the great hall. That cheered her slightly; perhaps no one would notice her in the confusion. Her feet hurt with every step, but that could be remedied later. For now, she would do what she had to.

She hobbled as quickly as she dared down the circular stairs to the great hall. Then she came to a teetering halt. Before her was a scene she was sure she would never forget.

Her brother stood there, along with Lothar and two strangers who stood with their backs to her. And around them all swirled a whirlwind that seemed to delight in blowing ashes from the fire into Lothar's face.

Lothar's servants stood all in a huddle at the back of the hall next to her. They made no sign of intending to stop her flight, but she supposed she should have expected nothing else. They might have been human at one time, those souls there, but they were that no longer. It was a terrified mass of creatures who shrank back against the wall when she looked at them, so she turned away, unwilling to torment them more.

Ehrne watched silently, his mouth agape, as Lothar and the older of the two strangers screamed at each other. Actually, Lothar was screaming. The older man stood there calmly, speaking every time Lothar would take a breath. This seemed to anger Lothar more each time, but somehow, with each firm word or two spoken by the older man, Lothar seemed to have less breath and vigor for shouting until all he was able to do was stand there with his mouth in an open scream and glare at the older man with hate in his eyes.

The other man, a younger one, stood with his hand upon the old man's arm, as if he leaned on him for strength, though she could not understand how that would be. She could not see his face, but he was possessed of a powerful form and stood straight and tall, as if he were someone to be reckoned with. The power that emanated from them both was like waves of heat from a fire; she could distinguish that even in her current state. Who were these two, then, to be dressed so humbly yet possess such power? Enemies Lothar had made long ago? Powerful noblemen fetched by Ehrne to come battle the foul mage and rescue her?

"Iolaire!"

She heard Ehrne's glad cry the moment before he ran across the hall to where she stood. He took hold of her and pulled her back with him toward the front door. She was almost all the way there before she managed to stop him with complaints over the condition of her feet. He swept her up into his arms and ran.

"But those men—" she protested.

"Will survive," he said curtly, "or they won't." He elbowed his way out the door and ran down the handful of steps to the ruined courtyard. He put her up onto a horse standing there unhappily. "Take my horse," Ehrne said. "I'll find something else to ride." He hesitated, then looked at another horse shifting restively nearby. "Are you man or beast?" he asked.

Iolaire stared at her brother, wondering if the journey from Ain-neamh had damaged his wits.

"Do you mind if I ride you?" Ehrne said uneasily.

The horse didn't answer. It looked at Ehrne as if it thought him daft as well.

Ehrne cursed, vaulted onto the horse's back and yelled at Io-laire to ride, and quickly, too. She did, regretting deeply not having thanked the men inside for making her escape fully possible.

She hoped they would know just the same.

I t was very late in the day when Ehrne finally allowed them to stop. Iolaire sat by the poor fire he'd built, shoving her numb, bare feet as close to the blaze as she dared. Ehrne dropped his cloak around her shoulders and sat down next to her. She looked at him.

"Ehrne —"

"Please, sister, not yet." He held his hands to the fire with his head bowed. It was quite some time that he sat there, silent and un-moving.

She understood. Any time spent in Lothar's hall was enough to render a body sick at heart. And if Ehrne were sitting next to her, not on his comfortable chair in their father's throne room, then that meant he had been banished as well. She reached out and put her hand on his arm.

"I'm sorry."

He looked at her quickly, then gave her a wan smile. "You have endured far worse than I, yet I begrudge you the ridding yourself of its burden. You must have things you wish to say, or questions to ask."

She nodded. "I do, actually. Why are you here? To rescue me?"

"That is part of it," he agreed. "The rest is complicated."

"I think I can wrap my mind around it," she said dryly, "if you say it slowly and simply."

He took a deep breath, looking uncharacteristically hesitant. "I was banished."

"Aye, I gathered as much."

"This is the complicated part." He paused. "You see, I tried to kill Morag."

"Mother?" she gasped. "But why?"

"Because, sister dear, she sold you to that black mage back there for money and the promise of power. I listened to her fix just such a bargain with him, but didn't realize whom she intended to betray until you went missing and I confronted her with my knowledge."

"And what did she say?"

"She admitted to it all with a callousness that still shocks me when I think about it."

"What did you do to her?" Iolaire asked faintly.

"I tried to stab her."

"Ehrne!"

He shrugged. "She's slipperier than you might expect. Father came upon me attempting the deed and cast me from our land. He was rather unwilling to listen to my tale."

She shivered. "What will happen to Sine and Artair? If you are not there to see to them and Father does not believe what you've told me, then where does that leave them? If Mother is capable of this offense to me, why not something similar to our younger siblings?" She looked off past the fire. "I can hardly believe it of her. How will we save them?"

"I do not know, given that the borders are closed to us," he said grimly.

Iolaire stretched forth her mind in an effort to take hold of the sense of her land. Before, before her time in Lothar's hall, it had been a continual stream of beauty and peace that ran through and under her thoughts. That connection with her land had been a part of her for as long as she could remember, coloring all her thoughts, her emotions, her desires.

It was gone.

'Twas no wonder her life seemed as bleak as Lothar's land had been.

"We should sleep," Ehrne said.

She looked at him wearily. "Are we safe?"

"If Lothar is vanquished, aye. If not, it matters not what we do, for we are all lost."

She nodded.

She understood completely.

S ymon spoke the last word of his own spell of binding, then hunched over with his hands on his thighs as he tried to catch his breath. The fact that his father was in much the same position made him feel slightly better.

"That will have to do," Yngerame gasped.

A stiff breeze blew Symon's hair into his eyes. With a curse, he grunted out another spell that left Hamil standing suddenly there, bouncing on his heels and looking far too lively for his own good.

"Well done," Hamil said, rubbing his hands together. "Very well done. Look at the fool, standing there with his mouth gaping open."

Symon managed to straighten and survey their handiwork. Lothar was trapped, mid-scream, and bound by so many unbreakable spells that he would have looked like a large, very plump chrysalis if the spells had been visible to any but those who had woven them about him.

"Well," he said, "all we can do is hope they hold."

"Even if he lives long enough to understand how the spells are fashioned," Yngerame said, straightening with an effort, "it will still take him years to unravel them all." He put his hand on Symon's shoulder. "Come, my son, and let us leave this awful place. It will be up to your children, I daresay, to see that his evil stays within its bounds. I am sorry for that, for I could not —"

Symon shook his head. "I could not kill him either, Father, much as he deserves it. We will just be vigilant."

"Aye, we will. Now, perhaps you would care to come to Wych-weald and rest after all this."

Symon considered. He would have something decent to eat for a change, if he went to Wychweald. He also might have a good look or two at that eleven princess he'd had the pleasure to mostly rescue, assuming she was there as well.

Aye, that was what he wanted—to sit at his mother's table and stare at a woman who had haunted his dreams for years and be no closer than he had ever been to having her, given the fact that he would still be unable to spew out two coherent words in her presence.

"I'd best return to Tor Neroche," Symon said with a sigh. "I do have a kingdom to see to."

"A decent meal, son," his father tempted.

Symon grunted. "You know, you could have gifted me a decent cook along with my crown."

"I thought to, but your mother feared you would find the combination of that lovely cabin and good food so pleasing that you would never return home."

Symon found it in him to laugh. "She knows I would have returned often."

"Then come now. Besides, I'll no doubt need help protecting that elf maiden young Ehrne of Ainneamh whisked away so quickly. It is a long road to Wychweald. I am quite sure you are just the lad to render such aid."

"You are a meddlesome old man."

Yngerame laughed. "I want grandchildren. Come with me at least for a few days. You can turn off the road at the great crossing easily enough if you decide otherwise."

"As you will," Symon agreed. "I've no stomach to argue with you."

"Ah," Yngerame said, slinging his arm companionably around Symon's shoulders. "I daresay even if you did, you wouldn't."

Symon started to follow his sire from the great hall when he caught sight of Lothar's servants standing in a terrified mass near the back of the hall. He paused. "Should we undo that?"

Yngerame frowned. "I don't know if it will serve them. The damage may be too great."

"Or it might not."

Yngerame looked at him. "Then let us try. Can you not do this?"

"You know I can, as you were the one to teach me how."

His father smiled. "My best pupil."

Symon chose a misshapen man and led him across the floor to the fire, under the watchful and blazing eyes of an immobile Lothar. He began to undo his brother's foul work—and that with great effort—but as he did so, he realized the changes were wrought so deeply and so poorly, that they could not be undone.

He kept at it, though it cost him dearly in energy and hope. When he was finished, the man was again a man but still quite damaged in mind and spirit.

Symon looked at his father. "You were right."

Yngerame shook his head slowly. "There was little hope from the start. I daresay there is no evil in them. When I return to Wychweald, I will find a steward for them. Then at least they will finish out their lives in some peace." He put his hand again on Symon's shoulder and led him toward the hall door. "Let us be away. I cannot bear to stand in this place of evil a moment longer."

Symon followed his father out into the winter sunshine and took a deep, cleansing breath. He used one last bit of precious energy to change his guards back from horses to men before he dragged himself over to his own horse. He found himself with no strength to mount.

"Symon."

He turned at his father's voice. The older man was smiling faintly, but his color was poor. Symon understood fully. "Aye?"

"Send the lads on ahead to look after Proìseil's children. I am not ashamed to desire a slower pace for a bit."

Symon did as his father requested, then heaved himself onto his own horse. He took a final look at his brother's ruined hall before he turned away and rode with his father away from the sea and into the peaceful, welcoming dusk.

I olaire rode next to her brother the following morning, cold, but grateful nonetheless for the pale winter sunshine. It was sublime to have not only liberty from Lothar's hall, but limitless freedom to do what she wished with the rest of her life.

At least she told herself it was so.

Something fell on her hands. She looked up, expecting to see rain clouds, but the sky was cloudless. She realized then that she was weeping. She looked down at her hands and watched them grow increasingly wet.

She took a deep breath. This would not do. There were many advantages to being banished. She would no longer have to endure those endless suppers where she was watched as covetously as a lone bottle of her father's rarest wine that was to be shared amongst the entire company. No longer would powerful elves from other families come to see if they could bluster their way into her father's good graces. Never again would she be forced to learn the languages of foreign kings so she could reject their suits in their own tongues. She was free to do what she liked, to converse with whom she cared to, to make a life where it suited her.

More tears fell.

The thought of never being allowed to return to Ainneamh was more devastating than she could bring herself to admit. How was she to go on? Where was she to go on *to*? Her life, her family, even her home was now forbidden her.

She dragged her sleeve across her eyes and cast about desperately for a distraction. She found one immediately in trying to divine the true identities of the half dozen men who rode in front of and behind her. Most of them had caught up with them the evening before, giving her a terrible fright. Ehrne had identified them as men-at-arms, though he had declined to name whom they served—as if that somehow was going to ease her mind more than knowing who commanded them.

Two other men had joined them as they broke camp that morning. She hadn't had a chance to converse with them—as they had kept firmly to themselves—but she had recognized them from the day before. She supposed she couldn't blame them for their silence, given that they had been the ones to deal whatever blow had been dealt to Lothar.

"Were they victorious, do you suppose?" she asked Ehrne quietly. "Those two who fought with Lothar?"

"Aye, else they wouldn't be here."

Iolaire looked at the back of the older man who rode a fair distance in front of her. "Who is he anyway? A renegade mage from the eastern lands you hired to help you?"

Ehrne looked at her with faint amusement. "Hardly. Don't you recognize him?"

"I doubt I would recognize Father in my current state," she said defensively.

"Well, that renegade mage, as you name him, is none other than Yngerame of Wychweald."

Iolaire caught her breath. "The wizard king of Wychweald," she breathed. "I never would have thought it. He does not look so powerful."

"Nor do I," Ehrne said loftily, "yet mortals quiver in fear before me."

She let that pass as she studied King Yngerame's back. "I've met him before. He looked younger then."

"He just battled his eldest son. Perhaps he's weary."

"I daresay."

"He's invited us to his palace," Ehrne continued. "I understand a body may enjoy uncommonly fine victuals there."

"Well, you'll be happy at least," she murmured, but she ceased quickly to listen to Ehrne recounting the rumors he had heard about the lady of Wychweald's supper table. She had other things to think on.

And to look at. She rode on for a very long time before she dared hazard a peek behind her. Closest on her heels, in front of the other half of the men-at-arms, rode the other man she'd seen with King Yngerame. He was weary as well, that she could tell from the set of his shoulders. She couldn't examine his features, though, thanks to the hood he had pulled close around his face.

"And what of that man back there?" she asked her brother casually. "Is he one of King Yngerame's retainers?"

Ehrne looked at her with his mouth open, then threw back his head and roared out a laugh that made her horse rear. She managed to bring the beast back under control, then glared at her brother. "Why is that amusing?"

Ehrne laughed again. "I must tell him. It will devastate him."

"Who is he, damn you for an empty-headed fool —"

"He is Symon, Yngerame's son," Ehrne said, grinning with a most inappropriate bit of humor. "Symon, the king of Neroche." He laughed again. "At least you didn't reduce him to a pig keeper. But I must tell him —"

"Do, and I will turn you into a toad."

His grin faded only the smallest bit. "You couldn't."

"I can and I will."

"I don't believe you."

She glared at him. "If you humiliate me by repeating my words, I will not only turn you into a toad, I will weave the spell so only I can undo it, I will carry you to a pond full of large, poisonous snakes, and I will not mourn your passing. And if you think I cannot do it, then think on all the times you snuck out of your lessons whilst I applied myself to them."

"You have spells to grow better smelling roses," he bluffed, "and nothing else."

"Blather on to him and see," she said.

He looked at her seriously, then pursed his lips. "I will think on silence."

"That might be wise." She looked at him once more to make certain he held her in the appropriate amount of awe, then turned her mind to what she'd just learned.

Symon of Wychweald, lately the king of Neroche, had come to rescue her.

"I went to him for aid," Ehrne supplied. "In case you wondered."

She tried to look uninterested. "Why to him?"

"Several reasons. One, he is Lothar's brother and has no love for him. Two, I assumed he had inherited some of his father's power and might be willing to use that power to aid me. And, lastly," he added, "he was the one monarch of the realm who had not fallen at your feet and begged for your hand upon seeing you. I thought that might be a boon."

"How so?" So, he had not wanted to have anything to do with her? She wondered if she should find that offensive or not.

"I determined that having my companion on a rescue ruining the rescue by pledging you undying love whilst he should have been about the business of freeing you might have been not only annoying but unproductive. I wanted him for his sword and his spells, not his spouting of wooing poetry at inopportune moments —"

"Ehrne?"

"Aye?"

"Shut up."

He closed his mouth, then huffed as he urged his mount forward where he commenced a spirited discussion with King Yngerame on the politics and corruptions of the schools of wizardry. Iolaire rode for quite some time in silence, giving thought to what she'd learned.

So, the king of Neroche had come to rescue her, quite possibly because he was the one man in the Nine Kingdoms who had no desire at all to seek her hand.

She wasn't certain how she should feel about that.

Well, no matter. She hadn't any more use for him than he apparently had for her. She had someone else in mind. And since she was no longer destined to wed with an elven prince, perhaps she would set herself the task of looking for that dark-haired, light-eyed man who had come to her father's hall. Finding him might take a goodly amount of time. And given that she had nothing but an excess of that on her hands, it seemed a task worthy of pursuit.

Still, it would be impolite not to at least thank the man behind her for his efforts, misguided though they might have been. She slowed her mount just a hair. In time, and over several miles, she managed to find herself riding next to the king of Neroche. She stole a look or two at him from under her hair—which was in sad need of a good brushing, but there you had it. It was difficult to look tidy after having been held captive without any of the appropriate creature comforts.

Symon's hands were strong, but graceful. She supposed he was equally proficient at wielding a sword or weaving a spell. A pity she knew next to nothing of him.

She knew a good deal about his father. Yngerame was as famous for his skill with magic as he was for his gilded tongue. He had not founded the schools of wizardry at Beinn òrain, but while still a student he had forged bonds between them that courses of study might be shared between the apprentices. He had mastered all the lessons available there, bested each of his masters in turn, and roamed far afield in exotic lands searching for strange and mysterious spells not known in the Nine Kingdoms. He had returned in time, wed himself the daughter of Murdach of Meith, built her a marvelous palace at Wychweald, then settled down to keep bees and dig in the dirt, shocking everyone who'd thought they'd known him. Iolaire had suspected, once she had learned his history, that his purposes were far deeper and more serious than weeding out the pea patch— though she had to admit she had always liked that about him, being something of a gardener herself.

But what of his son? She stole another look at Symon and wondered how much like his father he was. Was he equally skilled?

Was he kind or cruel? Was he like his brother, or not like him at all? These were questions worthy of an answer and since she had nothing to do until she was about her self-appointed quest to find that missing stranger, she would go ahead and ask him. But first a bit of small talk. She was certainly adept at that. She cleared her throat purposefully.

"Thank you," she said politely.

He didn't answer for quite a while. Then he slowly pushed his hood back from off his face and looked at her. "You are most welcome, Your Highness."

If she hadn't been such a good rider, she would have fallen off her horse.

It was him.

The man she had dreamed about since the night she'd first seen him.

Symon of Neroche. He had been near her all along, first at Wychweald, then as king of his own lands. And she hadn't known.

Symon of Neroche.

And he had come for her.

In a roundabout way.

She could only stare at him, speechless and unable to force herself to look away. He was as beautiful as she had remembered him being, gray with weariness though he might have been. His brow was just as noble, his face just as chiseled, his bearing just as regal.

And his eyes were blue.

A pale blue that was mirrored in the late afternoon winter's sky above them.

He was not smiling, but his look was pleasant, if not just the slightest bit inquiring, as if he wondered why it was she had not a useful thought in that empty head of hers. Iolaire wondered as well. There she was, the well-seasoned daughter of a powerful king who was used to smoothing over all sorts of diplomatic disasters and unacceptable proposals of marriage, yet she could not bring herself to spew forth two decent words that might make her sound something more than a fool.

"Ah," she managed, "ah, is this horse yours?"

Symon tilted his head to study her. "It is."

Well, he was economical in his speech, she would give him that. Perhaps she looked worse than she knew and he feared to overwhelm her in her current state of disarray. She smiled weakly. "I rode my brother's yesterday."

"Aye," Symon agreed with a solemn nod.

Iolaire had a thousand things to tell him, but every one of those things was completely daft. How could she say that though she had never spoken to him, she felt as if she had known him all her life? That he had haunted her dreams for years? That she had rejected suitor after suitor because they were not him?

He would think her mad.

But now he was here and she was free. She had to say something. There had to be a way to start the beginning of something she desperately wanted to grow and blossom like the beautiful, rare meadow-queen flowers in her father's most private garden. But she could not speak; she could not look away.

Disastrous.

"Do you breed horses?" she blurted out in desperation.

"Among other things."

Well, of course. He was the king of Neroche, after all. He likely had all sorts of kingly activities he went about each day. After all, Neroche was an enormous country. She'd paid attention long enough in her lessons to know that, at least.

He did not look away. Perhaps he had never seen a woman come undone in his presence as she was presently doing. She took a deep breath. She would have given herself a brisk slap, but who knew what that would lead him to believe. "I understand Yngerame of Wychweald is your sire."

He shifted in his saddle. "Aye, that he is."

Was he uncomfortable talking about his family, or had he decided she was too odd to tolerate? She sighed. "Well," she said finally, "at least you are nothing like your brother."

He looked at her with the faintest of smiles.

She could have sworn her mouth went dry. Aye, he was nothing like Lothar and somehow it had nothing and everything to do with his beauty. There was something else about him that bespoke steadiness in crisis, sureness in deed, unwavering loyalty in the face of criticism and libel. She could scarce believe he was not wed; Yngerame's list of potential brides for his son was almost as long as his list of what to plant in his garden and equally as famous.

"How so?" he asked.

"How so, what?" she asked.

"How so am I different from Lothar?"

"Oh," she said. "Well, he could not seem to stop talking."

And then she realized what she had said and how offensive it was. She shut her mouth with a snap.

But he laughed. It was a small laugh, but the sound of it fell around her like soft sunlight, warming and cheering her both.

"I must admit, Your Highness, that in your presence, words fail me."

Well, words might have failed him, but they certainly hadn't her. A pity the only words she could find to say reflected so poorly on all her years of princess training.

"Why? I am a woman just like any other."

He smiled again and shot her a look from under his eyebrows. The sight of it was so delightful and so unexpectedly charming, she felt a little unsteady and quite a bit more flushed than conditions outside warranted.

"You are not like any other," he said seriously.

She swallowed. "You would be surprised."

He only smiled and shook his head, but he seemed to settle more comfortably in his saddle and that small smile did not leave his face.

Iolaire felt the breath of beginnings wash over her. It was just a hint of the kind of spring she'd felt at home, but it was enough for now.

"May I continue to ride with you?" she ventured.

He looked at her for a moment or two in silence, then smiled again. "It would be my honor and pleasure, Your Highness, and surely more than I could dare hope for."

"See," she said, "you have words enough there."

He smiled again, but didn't reply.

Iolaire turned her face forward as well, though it fair killed her to do so. She told herself it did not matter, for she would possibly have days to look on him and marvel at the coincidence that had brought them together.

And for now, that was enough.

Five

Symon brushed his horse thoughtfully. It was a very unnecessary task—any of his men could have seen to it for him—but it gave him time to think. Perhaps that was an unhealthy and useless pursuit as well, but he couldn't seem to help himself.

Iolaire had thanked him.

She hadn't needed to, of course. Whatever else he might have been, he was Màire of Meith's son and as such knew his chivalric duty when it came to maidens in distress.

Though he suspected that fighting his brother for the treasure of Ainneamh hadn't been what his mother had had in mind all those years ago when she had ceaselessly drummed into his young heart the need to protect women and children from evil and hurt.

He would have to thank her, when next he saw her.

He stopped his grooming and peered over his horse's back to see what went on in their small camp. Iolaire was there, plodding about in boots that were several sizes too large. His boots, if anyone was curious. He'd brought them for no good reason he'd been able to divine at the time, but he was grateful for it now. At least Iolaire had something keeping her feet warm.

And given that he could hear her tromping from where he stood, at least he had a way to know where she was at all times. Not that he needed boots for that. Her very presence was a whisper of spring that seemed to brush over him whenever he was within a hundred paces of her. But since he now knew where she was and could gape at her as often as he liked without having to explain himself or make excuses for it, he did. Freely.

She was grace embodied, so drenched in beauty that he had a hard time looking at her, and he was not unacquainted with beautiful queens and princesses. Her hair was not much more tamed than it had been when he'd glanced at her in his brother's hall, but she had found some way to at least pin some of it back away from her face. He wasn't sure if that was a good thing or not. Staring at those fathomless blue eyes made him feel as if he were falling off a cliff, never to land, never to find his feet again.

Worse yet, he wasn't sure he wanted to.

She paced aimlessly, as if she suffered pain that could only be relieved by mindless movement. His heart ached for her. If he'd dared, he would have gone and offered her his companionship if for nothing more than what comfort it might provide.

And for the short time he could provide it. They were traveling slowly, but still the crossroads would be reached in a matter of days. He sighed. It was as he had told his father: He had no pressing reason to go to Wychweald and a handful of quite pressing reasons to return home. Therefore, three days alone remained before he had to either be about his duties as king or conjure up a decent reason to visit his father's hall.

Three days to drink in the sight of the eldest princess of Ainneamh.

Three days to wish he could look on her forever.

"A bit of swordplay, my liege?"

Symon jumped, then scowled at the suspiciously solemn captain of his guard who had appeared quite suddenly beside him.

"Not today, I don't think."

Hamil rolled his shoulders. "It would do you good. I always find that a bit of hard labor after serious magic is quite restorative."

"So says my father," Symon agreed sourly.

"A wise man, your father. A wise woman is your mother, as well." Hamil patted his chest meaningfully. "I have her bridal suggestions here still."

"Not interested," Symon said. He looked back toward the princess stomping about in his too-large boots. She said something to her brother, then walked away from the pile of wood Ehrne was having a hard time making burn. "I think I'm needed elsewhere."

Hamil looked at him pityingly. "Poor fool."

"I am your sovereign lord," Symon said. "Show some respect."

Hamil grunted. "Count yourself lucky I'm better with a sword than with spells, else you wouldn't have me at all." He patted his chest again and nodded knowingly. "When you're curious..."

Symon grunted, handed Hamil the curry comb, and walked back to camp. He paused next to Ehrne who was cursing quite inventively at green wood that simply would not light.

"Might I offer aid?" Symon asked.

Ehrne swore again. "What I need is dry wood. What my sister needs are boots that don't make a bloody ruckus every time she stomps next to me in them. Have you a solution to either?"

Symon watched Iolaire walking toward the woods. The boots were unwieldy, that he would admit, but he had no doubts that 'twas more than simply her gear that troubled her. She had passed an as-yet-undetermined number of nights in his brother's hall, and who knew what torments she had there suffered?

"She claims he did not touch her," Ehrne said quietly, rising to stand next to him, "yet still I see her much changed. She has lost her beauty, her fire, her passion for life."

"I pity us all if she finds any of the three," Symon muttered to himself, then reached down to toss a handful of dry grass on Ehrne's attempt at a fire. He called a flame from elements in the air and wrapped it firmly around the green wood.

The blaze began to burn quite cheerily.

Ehrne grunted. "A pity you cannot so easily do something about those boots."

"Who says I cannot?" Symon considered for a moment or two, then walked off into the forest. It took him a bit, but in time he found a patch of weeds plucky enough to survive the layer of snow. He chose what he needed, returned to sit down next to his fire, then began to weave.

"What are you doing?" Ehrne asked suspiciously.

"What does it look like I'm doing?"

"It looks, and I can hardly form the words due to my astonishment, as if you are weaving."

Symon did not look up. "And so I am."

"We are fugitives, out without proper escort, homeless, helpless, and hungry," Ehrne said, sounding increasingly incredulous, "and you choose to weave grass?"

Symon did look up then. "You aren't without proper escort," he pointed out mildly. "You have my men to guard you. My father has offered you refuge in his hall for as long as you'll have it, so you won't starve. Failing that, you have magic of your own." He looked back down at what he was doing. "Since you have complained so much about my boots, I am now making your sister a pair of shoes that fit."

"Out of grass?" Ehrne said in disbelief.

"Apparently," Symon answered. He wove a simple pattern that his mother had taught him one afternoon when he'd been ten, on an endless summer day before he'd left for the schools of wizardry at Beinn òrain. And as he wove, he considered the possibilities of Ehrne and Iolaire living at his father's hall.

They would be protected, that was true. They would be well fed and suitably entertained. Indeed, he suspected that it wouldn't be long at all before there was a line of mortals for each of them, mortals come to offer themselves as spouses to two such beautiful and desirable members of the elvish kingdom. Symon worked the final strands of grass into the slipper. Who was to say that Yngerame wouldn't offer to adopt the pair, so as to better see to matches for them?

Symon felt slightly queasy.

Of all the things he thought he might want of Iolaire of Ainneamh, becoming her brother was *not* one.

He set one bit of weaving aside and began a second before he could think any more.

Iolaire came to watch.

He knew this because the very air itself tingled when she walked through it. Symon kept on with his head bowed over his work, ignoring Ehrne's comments about his choice of pastimes and how his lack of skill would make itself apparent at any moment.

Iolaire, quite pointedly, bid him be silent.

At one point, Symon got up and went to roam in the meadow across the road from their camp. He had to search, but finally found a small handful of mountain flowers brave enough to poke through the snow. He returned, then stuck them into the shoes with as much artistry as he possessed, which wasn't much. He set the slippers down, then silently wove a spell of essence-changing over them.

Iolaire's breath caught. "Oh, how lovely."

Symon waited until the weariness passed before he picked up the shoes. Such spells, even for something so trivial, were not wrought without cost. He took a deep breath, waited until he thought his legs were up to the task of holding him, then rose. Even so, his hand shook a little as he handed the slippers to Iolaire. He was no artist, to be sure, but his magic and the beauty of the flowers compensated for it. He made Iolaire a low bow.

"I hope they please you, Your Highness."

"Illusion," Ehrne scoffed.

Iolaire shook her head. "I think not."

"They'll disintegrate into a pile of dead grass at an inopportune moment," Ehrne warned.

"Fool," Hamil said clearly from behind them, "can't you recognize a true change when you see one? And you with all your magic."

"'Tis but illusion," Ehrne insisted.

"Nay, it is not," Hamil said. "I've been around magic all my life and I know the difference."

Ehrne stared at Symon in shock. "But to learn to change the essence of a thing requires years of study, and…"

"And that coveted seventh ring of mastery," Hamil said smugly. "Now do you believe me?"

Ehrne looked a little pale. "Only a handful of men in this world have been so entrusted. Your father is one."

Symon looked at him as blandly as he could. "Aye, that is so."

"But you… you… you," he spluttered.

"He, he, he," Yngerame said, sounding quite amused as he walked into the clearing. "Symon is a legend in Beinn òrain, only surpassed by one other lad of equal skill who, I might add, managed to win all his rings of mastery in like manner, but at tender ten-and-six and not a score. Four years earlier, if anyone cares to count."

"And who is that other lad?" Ehrne asked in admiration.

"It was he himself, the immodest old fox," Symon said dryly. "Where have you been all these years, Ehrne?"

"Ducking out of his lessons," Iolaire supplied cheerfully.

Ehrne scowled, then looked at Symon. "Lothar's men were altered. How do you explain that? Did he learn the spells along with you?"

Symon shook his head. "He lost interest in the discipline of magic before he earned his first ring. Lothar suspects he may know a spell of essence changing, but he was not given it freely so who's to say? 'Tis my theory that he poached something from our good King of Wychweald's top desk drawer, the one with the lock that can only be opened by the three-headed key—"

"Or by a sharp knife wielded with fiendish determination," Hamil put in.

Yngerame smiled faintly. "Those are not spells that one dares write down, as you both know, so I daresay we can credit him with a goodly bit of eavesdropping on things that aren't what he believes them to be." He sighed. "At least we may count him well contained for the next few decades—or perhaps a pair of centuries if we did our work well. Then I'll trot out my old, tired self to see to him again. Until then, I'm off to hunt for supper. Anyone care to come along?"

"I'll come," Hamil said. "You set a fine table, sire, but I never quite trust your greens."

Yngerame put his hand on Hamil's shoulder and proceeded to give him a lecture on the virtues of all things bitter. Symon watched them walk off and thought again that his father looked more at ease than he had in years. A pity it had come at the cost of his elder son. Symon would have pondered the irony of that, but Ehrne seemed disinclined to allow him the peace for it.

"Why didn't *you* kill Lothar when you had the chance?" Ehrne asked.

Symon sighed. "My father could not and I could not do it in front of him. Perhaps later. For now, he is well bound."

"What does your sire mean when he says centuries?"

Symon smiled faintly. "Think you that only elves live a thousand years?"

"You do not."

"We'll see, won't we?"

Ehrne merely looked at him, silent, as if he simply could not take another shocking revelation.

Symon looked at Iolaire who was holding up the hem of her gown to look at her shoes. "Do they please you, lady?"

"Greatly," she said, looking at him with a smile. "Thank you."

He felt, quite suddenly, much like a deer frozen in a meadow in the face of a hunter. He searched for something to say, something charming, something amusing, something coherent even, but found that, as usual, just the sight of her was too much for him. Maybe 'twas best he would never have her. It would have been a very silent marriage.

"Shall we hunt for berries?" she asked. "For a sweet after the meal. I fear that after last night, I too have grave doubts about your father's greens." She shivered delicately. "Passing bitter."

Symon struggled briefly, then gave up on speech and contented himself with a nod.

"Ehrne, tend the fire," Iolaire instructed, taking Symon by the hand. "The king of Neroche and I will return later."

"Do not become over friendly with him," Ehrne warned. "He is not—ow, damn you!"

Symon saw the rock stick for the briefest of moments between Ehrne's eyes before it dropped down into his lap. He looked at Iolaire and had to laugh.

"You are dangerous."

"You've no idea. Best come along then, lest I turn my wrath upon you."

He laughed a little more, mostly to himself, and mostly because it kept him from being completely undone by the feeling of Iolaire of Ainneamh's fingers entwined with his. To be sure, he was a man full grown, and he was not unacquainted with the ways of men and women. He had managed bouts of half-hearted wooing at his father's command, to useful and well-bred princesses and wizardesses of good repute.

All of that meant nothing now. He was walking through a forest still sleeping under winter's spell, falling under the spell of an elven princess who seemed not to notice that he was as tongue-tied as a bastard village lad come to his lord's castle for the first time.

"I'm sorry," he said, when he thought he could spew out two words in succession and succeed.

"About what?" she asked.

"That you were there," he said slowly. "And that you cannot return home."

She smiled gravely. "I thank you for your words, but do not pity me overmuch. Freedom is more greatly prized after it is lost for a time." She looked off into the distance, but seemed not to see what was before her. "It is some small comfort, that freedom."

He couldn't imagine. He had never been barred from his home, never not found a way to be welcomed wherever he went. And though he loved his father's hall, he had spent a goodly part of his life in other places and did not find traveling unpleasant.

He very much suspected Iolaire had never been outside Ainneamh. She had lost not only her home, but also the pleasure in her memories of her past and her dreams for the future.

"Poor girl," he murmured, then realized what he'd said. He was digging for words of apology when she smiled at him and squeezed his hand.

"No matter," she said. "I am free, with my life before me and all things possible."

He could say nothing. His heart, overused thing that it was, was too full of her loss.

"I begin to wonder," she said, tilting her head to look at him sideways, "if it is because you do not like me that you find nothing to say."

"Nay," he managed. "Nay, that is not the reason."

"Good," she said, then she turned her attentions to what was before them. "Ah, look over there. Wintergreen. Just what your father's salad needs."

And she was just what he needed. He still was not convinced he would have her, but he had also never expected to be hunting berries with Proìseil the Proud's most beloved daughter.

As she had said, like was before her and all things were possible.

He wondered if he dared believe that for himself as well.

Six

❖

"What, by Uisdean of Taigh's glittering crown, do you think you are doing?"

Iolaire didn't move from where she sat on a log, resting her chin on her fists, which rested on her knees so she might more easily observe the two men exercising in the open field before her. But she did condescend to glance her brother's way. "What does it look like I'm doing?"

"It looks as if you're contemplating having some sort of, oh, I don't know, *liaison* with that man."

"Which man? The one who wove me slippers from grass and made them beautiful with his own generosity? The one who has endured your vile complaints for longer than he was obligated to and should likely turn you into a burr under his saddle except that it would irritate his good horse?" She looked up at him mildly. "That man over there?"

Her brother folded his arms over his chest and pursed his lips. "Swordplay is so pedestrian."

"You engage in it."

"It becomes a thing of magnificence when I apply myself to it."

She laughed. "Ehrne, you pompous ass, get you gone and cease distracting me. I've business here."

He squatted down next to her. "Iolaire, do not give your heart," he said seriously. "There must be a chance to return home. I daresay you will not endear yourself to Father if you try to do so with a mortal scampering at your heels."

A dreadful hope bloomed and died almost before she could breathe in and out. "Ehrne, we will not be allowed in, no matter if I bring Symon or not. And in case you've overlooked it, I suspect our good king of Neroche isn't quite all as mortal as he seems. I daresay even you didn't manage to sleep through *all* of Master Cruinn's lectures on the genealogies of the Nine Kingdoms."

Ehrne grunted. "I'm uninterested and I will still say you should leave him be."

"I'm not doing anything with him," she said easily. "Just talking."

He pursed his lips, rose, and walked away. Iolaire watched him go, then turned back to the exercising going on in the well-trampled meadow in front of her. It didn't continue much longer, which did not displease her. It was a pleasure to watch Symon hoist a sword like any other man of substance; it was even more pleasant to have him pay her heed like any other man of good breeding.

Never mind that sometimes he looked at her, when he thought she wasn't looking, in a way that made her want to sit down.

It made her, against all odds, forget even for the briefest of times, the pain of her banishment. And given that such was a gaping wound in her heart that she feared would never heal, the distraction of Symon was something to be prized indeed.

The king in question resheathed his sword, then exchanged a few pleasantries with his captain before he tromped across the field and stopped in front of her.

"You look well."

"Winter's chill suits me somehow," she said with a smile. "It helps that my slippers seem to carry a hidden warmth. I wonder if that is a happy accident?"

"I should think not," he admitted. "But who's to say? If they please you, then I am pleased." He hesitated. "Perhaps you would care to walk a bit before we break camp? These long rides can be wearying."

She nodded and rose with a smile. Soon, she was crunching along a snowy road with him, looking down at the beautiful, flowered slippers that seemed to dissolve the snow whenever they touched it so she walked upon dry ground. She looked up at Symon walking next to her and couldn't help a smile. He was handsome, aye, but more than that he was just genuinely himself, unlike so many men who had courted her. He gave her gifts apparently without expecting anything in return, and merely because it pleased him to do so. He would have baffled her sire. She knew he confused Ehrne quite thoroughly.

She liked that about him.

"So," she said, stepping over a particularly slushy patch of road, "what is it you do each day?"

"Tend horses. Much out stalls. Stoke fires."

"In between entertaining envoys from other powerful kingdoms?" she asked politely.

"Aye, well," he said deprecatingly, "I generally invite them to pick up a pitchfork and dig right in with me."

She laughed. "Much like your sire, I see. He is notorious for forcing the mighty ones to putter with him in his pea patch."

"I admire my father very much," Symon admitted. "And his techniques seemed to have worked for him."

"He is a powerful mage," Iolaire ventured. "Perhaps they feared to incur his wrath so they humor him."

She waited, but he neither agreed nor disagreed with her. He also didn't offer any comparisons of his own power to his father's. She studied him surreptitiously. She had seen him in Lothar's hall, but it had been his father weaving the spell to bind Lothar—or so she had assumed. If Symon knew spells that would change the essence of things, then he must be powerful indeed.

But somehow, despite that, he did not look it. He looked like a man who might happily muck out his stables then return inside and desire nothing more than a hot super and a blazing fire. Did men fear him or did he have trouble with the ambassadors who came his way?

"You're staring at me with a frown," he remarked.

"I should know more of the outside world," she admitted, "and more about the souls who people it. It is a very easy thing to be comfortable in my land and never wonder what goes on outside it."

"Were you not required to learn anything of mortal kings?" he asked.

"Aye, I was. I learned much of your father."

"I take it you were off on holiday the day they discussed me?" But he laughed as he said it. "It is unimportant. I am but a small cog on a very large wheel."

"Are you?" she mused. She looked down at her slippers again. It occurred to her that if this man could take notice of a banished elven maid's cold feet and use his gifts to ease her discomfort, then his land and the people dwelling thereon were fortunate to have him. She looked up at him. "I daresay not."

"Thank you"

She laughed a bit shakily. "I cannot imagine my opinion matters much."

"You would be surprised," he said dryly. He smiled down at her as he walked with his hands clasped behind his back. "Nay, Neroche is vast and it requires much effort to tend it properly. I feel hardpressed to see to it all."

"Your land is beautiful, even under winter's chill," she offered.

He smiled a little ruefully. "Winter is hard here, but Neroche is beautiful even then. It is not Ainneamh, of course, but there is much about it that is lovely and grand. We've a long, beautiful coastline to the west, mountains to the north and south, and beautiful valleys scattered throughout. I daresay I haven't traveled over as much of it as I would like. A king should know the vales and hamlets that are in his care, don't you think?"

She nodded. How would it be to wander that land with him, binding the little boroughs and villages together, coming to know the people who would depend on him for their safety and security? Would he make shoes of grass for small children or bind up cracks in kettles for women who had no men to see to it for them?

All of a sudden, a vision of a freshly plowed field came to her, replete with the smells of spring and possibility. Symon's land waited for the seeds of a new reign to be planted and the touch of the king's hand to do it. How much better would it be if there were a queen to set things to growing as well? That feeling of possibility, of laboring with her hands for something she had cultivated herself—it was almost enough to take her breath away.

"Iolaire?"

She closed her eyes briefly. Ah, the way he said her name, as if he found it beautiful. She looked at him and smiled.

"Aye, my king?"

He smiled. "You were very far away."

She shook her head. "I think I begin to understand why your father spends so much time in his vegetable garden."

"I should think you do. Your land is lush and verdant as well."

She smiled, even though she thought she might have preferred quite suddenly to weep. Symon took her hand and held it in his.

"Forgive me, Iolaire," he said. "I did not mean to grieve you."

"You did not grieve me," she said with a wan smile. "I cannot forever avoid speaking about it. The truth of it is, I will have to make a new home—"

A voice called from behind them. Iolaire looked over her shoulder to see her brother shouting at them and waving for them to return.

Symon sighed. "They are ready, it seems."

She nodded and turned with him back to where their company

was waiting. "How much longer until we reach Wychweald, do you think?"

"Three days," he said.

"You sound quite sure of that," she said, faintly amused. "Are you so eager to reach your mother's cooking pot?"

He paused for such a long time that she began to wonder if she'd said something amiss.

"Symon?"

"I'm not going to Wychweald," he said finally.

"You aren't?"

"We'll reach the crossroads tomorrow. I must turn aside from this road then."

She felt foolish for being caught so by surprise. Of course he wouldn't go to his father's hall. He had his own kingdom, his own hall, his own affairs to see to. Perhaps he had a woman to woo and had been interrupted in his plans by Ehrne's insistent demands for aid.

She slipped her hand from his. "Of course," she said with a brightness she most certainly did not feel. "You must miss your hall."

"There isn't much to miss," he admitted. "'Tis my father's hunting lodge. It is, as your brother might say, a hovel."

"Ignore him. He has no imagination."

Symon stopped suddenly. "'Tis no place for a queen, to be sure."

She looked at him blankly. Why should she care whether or not his hall was sufficient for him to take a bride there? Indeed, she began to hope the bloody roof leaked—

"I will build you a palace," he said, taking her hands. "In the valley of Chagailt, where 'tis warmer." He paused. "It rains a great deal there, so I understand."

Iolaire blinked. "A palace?"

"Aye, a palace. A beautiful palace made of granite from the hills of Iarmil, fine furnishings carved by the dwarves of Sgùrr, tapestries woven by the wizardess Nimheil, who dyes her yarn with her own tears—"

She found words had failed her entirely. Was he proposing to

her? Where were the other women she'd been certain he was planning to woo?

"Are you a gardener?" She heard words and realized belatedly
that she was the one to speak them. He was going on about priceless
wonders, and she was wondering if he needed someone to scratch in
the dirt for him?

"A gardener?" he asked blankly.

Well, there was no sense in not continuing down that path to
true madness. He was already looking at her as if she'd lost what
few wits remained her; she might as well give him more reason to
believe it.

"Do you need a gardener?" she asked.

He frowned, as if he actually spared the effort to try to understand what she was getting at.

"You didn't mention gardens," she finished lamely.

A corner of his mouth twitched.

"I amuse you," she stated.

"Nay," he said slowly, "nay, 'tis a fair question. But actually, I
was more concerned with putting some kind of roof over your head
than I was with shrubberies and such, but gardens would be lovely
as well."

"A roof over my head?"

"That is usually what a husband sees to, is it not?"

"A husband?"

"Aye."

"Is this a proposal of marriage?"

"Am I doing it so poorly?"

In all honesty, she'd had so many proposals over the course of
her majority that she'd long since ceased to give them more thought
than was required in order to reject them.

"It was lovely," she said honestly. "Truly."

"It was spur-of-the-moment," he admitted.

Iolaire would have listened more closely but her brother was
beginning to shout at her quite frantically. She motioned impatiently
for him to be quiet.

"A proposal," she said to Symon. "Well—"

"I never thought to ever blurt out the words," he said, "given that I thought I would never stand this close to you—"

Ehrne was almost beside himself now. Iolaire swore at him loudly, then turned to Symon. "What did you say?"

"I said I never thought to even stand so close to you without your father taking a sword to me for my cheek—"

"Which I will do, mage king," said a voice from her right, "if you do not stand aside."

"Father!" Iolaire said, turning around with a gasp. She could scarce believe her eyes. Now she understood why Ehrne had been so distraught. "Father, what are you doing here?"

"Saving you from a life of misery," Proìseil said promptly. "Neroche, release her."

Iolaire didn't give Symon the chance to do it on his own. She let go of his hands and stood between him and her father, lest her sire use that sword hanging at his side for unwholesome and untoward purposes.

"He came for me when you would not," she said, pointedly. "And for that I am grateful."

"Your gratitude does not need to extend to binding yourself to him," Proìseil said sternly. "Besides, I've come to fetch you home. I have convinced all those necessary that banishment was unjust. It is lifted."

She swayed. Indeed, she suspected she might have landed quite unsteadily on her backside had she not swayed back into Symon. He steadied her with his hands on her shoulders. When he would have released her, she reached up and put her hands over his.

"He is building me a palace," she said weakly. "With fine stone-work and carvings. Tapestries by Nimheil. I plan to make the gardens the envy of the Nine Kingdoms."

Proìseil snorted. "How can that possibly compare to Ainneamh, where there is beauty as far as the eye can see, music that touches the soul, those of your family about with whom you have had association all your days! Will you give all that up for that mortal there?"

Iolaire looked over her shoulder at Symon, but he was steadily regarding her father, his expression inscrutable. Iolaire turned back to her sire.

"And if I choose him?"

Her father's expression told of his determination. "We do not wed with mage's get."

"But what of Sgath—"

"Do not speak to me of others," Proìseil said curtly. "Here is a horse, Iolaire—"

"What of me?" Ehrne said suddenly from behind her. "Do you have a horse for me as well?"

Proìseil glared at his eldest son. "You tried to murder your mother."

"She deserved worse."

"Well, she'll have it," Proìseil said grimly, "but not from you. As for your fate, I've not decided yet. Grace Wychweald with your delightful presence until I come to a decision." Proìseil then looked at Iolaire. "Well?"

She looked down. She saw her slippers and thought of Symon. Granted, she had only known him a few days; she had dreamed of him for far longer than that.

But to return to Ainneamh...

Without him.

She took a deep breath, put her shoulders back and lifted her chin. She did not dare look at either her father or her love.

"I will go—"

"Home," Symon interrupted.

Iolaire whirled around to look at him. "What?"

"You will go home," he said.

"But I thought—"

He pulled her into his arms and held her tightly. She could have sworn he trembled, just once. He buried his face in her hair, then he spoke against her ear.

"Go with your father."

"You do not want me," she managed.

"I want you more than I desire my own life, and for far longer than it will be granted me, but I cannot keep you from Ainneamh."

She could say nothing. *Home.* All that she held dear, all that she knew, the only place she had loved...

"Take him at his word, Iolaire," Symon said quietly, "and return with him."

"Well spoken," Proìseil said. "I will credit the king of Neroche with sense in this matter. Now, Neroche, get you back to your father's cabin of wattle and daub and allow me to take my daughter back to the magnificence she's accustomed to."

Iolaire turned to her father. "He rescued me. You owe him at least a supper in thanks."

"I'll think on it."

She turned and threw her arms around Symon's neck, hugging him tightly. "I will miss you," she said, her voice cracking.

"I will come for supper," he whispered into her hair, "and then we will discuss plans for your gardens."

She nodded, then sank back down on her heels. She looked into his pale eyes and saw her own torment mirrored there. She wanted home; she wanted him. He wanted her; he could not keep her from the place that would heal her heart.

Symon released her finally and took a step or two backward. "My heart is glad for your chance to return to the land you love," he said with a grave smile.

"You will come soon," she said, not making it a question.

"He will come at my invitation," Proìseil put in immediately, "and I suggest he not waste his time watching for my messenger."

Iolaire turned and with a deep sigh walked to her father's company.

She watched her shoes as she did so.

Flowers bloomed on her slippers, but she wondered how they would ever bloom again in her heart.

Seven

S ymon stared off after Iolaire as she rode with her father's company southward. He wanted to believe he'd done the noble thing. Indeed, how could he have done otherwise?

"Well, are you going to just stand there, or are you going to go after her?"

Symon smiled at his father. "I'm thinking."

Yngerame laid his hand briefly on Symon's shoulder. "The reason you matriculated through all the schools of wizardry so quickly is because you are quick of hand and of thought. But, my son, in this, I tell you that you think too much."

"I haven't yet begun to truly contemplate this."

"The world will tremble when you do," Ehrne said. He shook his head with a sigh. "I cannot believe you let her go."

Symon looked at him archly. "You wanted me to."

"That was before I resigned myself to the fact that she loves you," Ehrne said with pursed lips. "Not even the incomparable wonders of Ainneamh can root that out of her poor breast."

"Well, apparently your father left me you in trade."

Ehrne snorted, but declined to reply.

"And fortunately so," Symon continued, "as I've a question or two to put to you."

"Then unpack the luncheon gear," Ehrne said, flexing his fingers purposefully. "I have a feeling I'll need a little something to tuck into as you pepper me with questions I will likely find unpalatable."

Symon smiled briefly. "Later. Answer me this first: What exactly are the laws of banishment?"

"I've had more experience with them of late than I ever thought to," Ehrne grumbled, "but as I understand it, once an elf leaves Ainneamh that elf may not return. Unless they go for diplomatic reasons, of course," he added. "But we have as little traffic as possible with you lowly mortals. Dulls the blood, you know."

Symon ignored Hamil's very loud snort. "It seems harsh," he said thoughtfully, "to forbid your family entry back into their home for such simple things."

"Aye, but it has been done, and more than once, without any remorse. Witness Sgath, who wed with Eulasaid of Camanaë. I daresay he longed for home, but his banishment was never lifted." Ehrne paused. "Do you know their tale?"

"Only that they were wed and Ainneamh mourned," Symon said. "Sgath was your father's brother, was he not?"

"He was. He was out riding one day when he found Eulasaid fleeing from ruffians chasing her along the border of Ainneamh. He took her back to the palace, gave her refuge, and fell in love with her."

"And how could he not?" Yngerame asked. "She was, and still is, a remarkable woman. As you may or may not know, Eulasaid is the one who expelled Lothar from Beinn òrain when he overstepped his bounds." Yngerame shook his head in admiration. "Her power is luminous. I daresay Sgath loves her more today than he did when he wed her, and he loved her greatly then to give up his home."

"I daresay you might have it aright," Ehrne agreed, "though the giving up of his home wasn't exactly his choice."

"Then he was banished as well?" Symon asked.

"It was a failed attempt at trying to remain in both worlds, the mortal and the immortal. Sgath convinced his brother the king to come riding with him. When they reached the border, Sgath stood half in Ainneamh, half out, and Eulasaid claimed him for her own."

"Romantic," Symon noted.

"And off by about ten paces," Ehrne said dryly. "They misjudged the border that badly, you see. I smile now, but 'twas a tragedy that provided fodder for Ainneamh's bards for years. My father banished Sgath on the spot. The banishment has remained in force, even through the succession of kings."

"Interesting," Symon said, calculating furiously. It wasn't as if Eulasaid had possessed a good map to determine where the border was. Sgath should have known, of course, but perhaps he had been distracted—

"'Tis likely for that reason that my father is so unwilling to see Iolaire go with you," Ehrne said with a sigh. "He has not spoken to Sgath since that day. Perhaps there is a place in that hard heart of his that grieves at the thought of never having speech with my sister again—even if that would be his choice and not hers."

Symon rubbed his hand over his face. "If I manage to claim Iolaire on the border, then she will be allowed to come and go as she pleases?"

"It has never been successfully done, but aye, in theory that is the case."

Symon frowned at Ehrne. "Does your father not consider the fact that perhaps Iolaire might *want* to wed me?"

"He no doubt thinks time away from her land has dimmed her wits," Ehrne said. "Besides, you are mage's get." He shot Yngerame a faintly apologetic look.

Yngerame only smiled easily. "What your father refuses to see is that Symon is his equal in every respect."

"Ha!" Ehrne exclaimed, then fell silent.

"Am I?" Symon said with a smile. "I daresay not, Father, though the comparison flatters me."

"You forget your genealogy, my son."

"Perhaps our good elven lordling might like to hear a recounting of it," Hamil said.

"Perhaps you should attend to that light afternoon tea first," Ehrne suggested.

"I'll be brief," Hamil said. He made himself comfortable on a fallen log. "There was once a lad from a small, obscure village called Wychweald. He was deft-handed and quick-tongued and when he talked the lowest master of the school of Wexham into letting him attend on a trial basis, he began on his path to greatness."

Ehrne sighed deeply and sought a seat on a rock.

"As you might or might not know, being from Ainneamh and all, and as I may or may not have told you already," Hamil continued, "our good King Yngerame won all seven rings of mastery from the schools of wizardry by the time he was ten-and-six. Having nothing more to learn there, he went in search of other knowledge in strange and diverse places. And when that search yielded nothing of interest, he began to create his own magic. And it was whilst he was about his labors that he wandered into the kingdom of Meith and saw Màire of Meith walking along the shore near her father's palace."

"Màire of Meith," Ehrne repeated faintly. "Granddaughter of Sìle of Tòrr Dòriann."

"Tòrr Dòriann being that little village on Ainneamh's eastern borders, if memory serves," Hamil said blandly. "Do I have that aright?"

Ehrne nodded weakly. "Iolaire hinted Symon bore elven blood, but I feared that blow to her head had done more damage than I feared."

"You were wrong," Hamil said bluntly. "But now back to our tale. Yngerame asked King Murdach of Meith if he could have his daughter to wife. I believe his reply was something akin to 'Come home, daughter, without this worthless mortal here.' Or it could have been merely 'ha!' bellowed with great disdain."

Ehrne snorted out a laugh. "Indeed."

"Meith also added that he would be damned if he would give his beloved daughter to a landless, less-than-well-scrubbed wizard of no repute. Of course, our good king who was not king yet had reputation enough, but Meith had arrogance to match, so they were at an impasse. Yngerame promised Màire that he would return for her when he had satisfied her father's demands, then set off to see to that satisfying. He happened a few weeks later upon Petier of Neroche and challenged him to a game of draughts, with Neroche as the prize. Actually, King Petier would have preferred to have had the changing of his mother-in-law into a set of fire irons as the prize, but Yngerame did place certain limits upon the use of his powers."

Symon smiled to himself as Hamil warmed to his tale.

"Now, as you might guess," Hamil continued, his eyes alight with pleasure, "Yngerame won that game of draughts fairly. Neroche surrendered his vast territory, which included that little village of Wychweald, and went to stay with his quite lively and unquiet mother-in-law in her manor house, miserable to his dying day. Yngerame, quite content with his victory, returned to Meith and asked if it were enough."

"I take it King Murdach said aye, when the alternative was no doubt gracing Wychweald's most elaborate hearth as fire tools himself?" Ehrne asked with half a smile.

"He did," Hamil agreed, "though he complains about it to this day."

Symon yawned. "I thank you for the tale, Hamil. It was quite instructive. I, for one, am grateful for my mother's choice."

"Speaking of your mother, I still have her list here if you're interested," Hamil said. "To take your mind off Princess Iolaire."

Symon ignored him and turned to Ehrne. "So if I am to succeed, she must be in both kingdoms."

"So I would expect."

"And I wonder how I'll possibly ask her to do that without your father rushing off with her before I can claim her."

"I've no idea, but I don't suppose you could turn me into a little bird to sit on her shoulder while you try, could you?"

Symon smiled. "I'm going for a walk. I'll need peace to think on this."

"I cannot believe you're not the least bit curious about your mother's suggestions," Hamil said.

Symon sighed. "Very well, to silence you once and for all upon the matter." He took the list Hamil produced, read it, then handed it back with a smile. "One name," he said. "Read it yourself."

Hamil did so. He looked at Symon and laughed. "Iolaire of Ainneamh."

"A wise woman, your mother," Yngerame said with a nod. "Very wise indeed."

"And to think I carried this for this long for no reason," Hamil said. "I'm surprised it didn't blow off me whilst I was that ill wind about its foul business."

"If it eases you any," Symon said with a smile, "hers would have been the only name on my list, if I had possessed the courage to make one." He started to walk away, then stopped and looked at his captain. "An ill wind," he said. "Well, that is something to think on."

"Turn me into a leaf and carry me along," Ehrne begged. "I must see this. Perhaps you can claim me as well and save me from a life in this dreary bit of world."

"Claim you as what?" Hamil snorted. "His squire?"

"I'm desperate enough to consider it," Ehrne said.

Symon exchanged a smile with his father, then walked away, leaving Hamil and Ehrne arguing over what form would suit him best.

The wind stirred in the trees.

Symon smiled.

Eight

❖

Iolaire rode beside her father, feeling with every beat of her horse's hooves that she was going in the wrong direction. She wanted to see Ainneamh again, truly she did. But she didn't want to be put again to market, no matter her father's great sacrifice in coming to fetch her. She didn't want an elf, no matter his beauty; she didn't want a wizard, no matter his power; she didn't want a king from the east beyond the Nine Kingdoms, no matter his exotic strangeness nor the fathomless depths of his purse.

She wanted a man whose boots were worn, whose clothes were serviceable, whose fingernails showed telltale signs of being familiar with the dirt of his realm.

A gentle breeze whispered over her suddenly.

She caught her breath, then lifted her face to the sun. She smiled for the first time in days. The breeze encircled her, enveloped her with a joyousness that stole her breath, then made her laugh from the delight of it.

He had come for her.

And if this was what it felt like to be loved by Symon of Neroche, then she had chosen well indeed.

You will soon come to the border of your land, the wind whispered to her. *You must have one foot in Ainneamh, one in Neroche.*

And just how was she to see that, she wondered. She allowed herself the consummate pleasure of being enveloped by that sweet breeze and supposed she would know when the time came.

If you're willing...

Iolaire smiled to herself.

The wind swirled around her, ruffled her hair gently, then flung itself before her.

Iolaire waited a few moments before she reined her horse in. "Father, I must walk for a bit."

Proìseil looked at her kindly. "As you will daughter. I daresay it has been a trying few days."

She had a twinge of regret at her subterfuge, but she squelched it. She loved her father and when he wasn't about his business of being king, he was the kindest of men. But her heart had been given and that to a man who was never just king and never just a man, but always Symon. Whatever she had to do to be his, she would do.

She dismounted and walked a little ways until she saw in front of her a very thin silver line that shimmered upon the snow. She stopped and very carefully put one foot in her old home and kept on in her new.

The breeze blew about her father, stirring leaves and his cloak, then stopped to swirl fiercely in a space ten paces before him. The whirlwind became Symon. He stood there with his hair wind-blown and a wildness in his eyes that should have given her father pause. True to himself, Proìseil merely drew up and scowled.

"You are in my way, mage king."

"And you are leaving Neroche with something that's mine," Symon answered.

Proìseil sniffed. "I will not wed my daughter to a lowly wizard—"

Symon strode forward, took Iolaire by the hand, and looked up at her father unflinchingly. "I now claim Iolaire of Ainneamh for my

own while she stands in my land and yours. I do it in accordance
with your law which was before you took the throne and will remain
after you have given that throne to another. And thus it is done."

Iolaire looked at her father to find him gaping at Symon in astonishment. Then his expression darkened. He shut his mouth with
a snap.

"Damn you."

"Father!"

Proìseil glared at Symon. "You may *not* have her."

Symon merely lifted one eyebrow, but said nothing.

Iolaire watched her father with fascination, wondering what he
would do now. He continued to glare at Symon, as if by his very
look he could force him to give up. It took several minutes of quite
uncomfortable and very charged silence before Proìseil actually sat
back in his saddle, cursed quite inventively, and heaved a gusty sigh.
He scowled at Iolaire.

"I suppose if he is that clever, he deserves his heart's desire." He
fixed Symon with a steely look. "I assume she is your heart's desire.
If not, you will find yourself quite unable to wed her, whether or not
you've claimed her."

"Father!" Iolaire exclaimed again. She looked at Symon and felt
that same joyous breathlessness wash over her. "You came for me."

"I apologize it was not sooner," Symon said. "I had to wait until
you reached the border."

She shook her head. "It does not matter. Now, my liege, shall
you wed me in Ainneamh, or in your father's lodge in the mountains?"

Her father began to splutter.

"I would wed you in the vale of Chagailt, but I would begrudge
myself the time it took to build a palace there," Symon said. "I will
wed you where you choose —"

"It is *not* her choice," Proìseil cut in loudly.

Iolaire looked at him. And for once, he paused, considered, then
relented.

"Mount up," her father said wearily. "Neroche, meet us in my hall in a month's time. All will be ready."

Symon inclined his head. "I thank you for the honor you do me, not only in the gift of your daughter, but by allowing me inside your hall."

"How else am I to see my grandchildren in times to come, damn you? Iolaire, come. We'll go home."

Symon kept hold of her hand. "I will see her there."

Proìseil scowled. "'Tis a very long ride and you have no horse."

"We won't be riding."

Iolaire looked at him. "We won't?"

"Have you ever shapechanged?"

Proìseil's eyes bulged and his face turned an alarming shade of red. "Elves do not..." he spluttered. "They most certainly would never... ever..."

Iolaire caught her breath. "I've never tried. Do you think I can?"

"You are Proìseil of Ainneamh's daughter," Symon said with a smile. "I daresay there is little you cannot do." He pulled her farther down the path away from her still protesting father. "Here is the spell..."

Iolaire looked back over her shoulder to find her father looking as if he might explode at any moment. She whispered Symon's spell along with him, then suddenly found herself blowing through the leaves of the trees, intertwining with the wind that was the king of Neroche.

And then she somehow lost her grasp of who she was. She became the breeze rustling through the trees of the forest, transparent as the sun filtering through her, carrying with her the scents of flowers and pines and the calls of eagles that soared above her. And all the while, Symon was there, around her, woven through her, bearing her aloft.

She thought she might perish from the joy of it.

Nine

Symon stood in the king of Ainneamh's hall with a breath-stealingly beautiful elven princess by his side and wondered several things.

One, was it possible for him to have imagined as he visited this selfsame hall years earlier that he might at some future time again walk over that floor of polished midnight-colored marble only this time as the groom of an elven maid?

Two, would he survive a lifetime spent looking at the lovely, remarkable woman standing at his side?

Three, would Proiseil survive the ceremony, or would his heart fail him before it was finished?

Symon felt Iolaire take his hand and he smiled down at her. The past month had been beyond what he'd expected. They had laid out the palace of Neroche at Chagailt. They had roamed over his land in whatever shape Iolaire, who had proved to have a magic easily as strong as his, had fancied.

They had already begun to visit his people, going wherever they had felt needed. Symon had watched with awe and a full heart

as Iolaire had bestowed her radiant smiles on noblemen and poor
farmers alike. She had welcomed children of all classes and states of
cleanliness into her arms and onto her lap, drawing them close and
showing them the beauty of their lives and their land in the way only
she could see it, she who had grown to love it as much as he, Symon,
did.

And then they had retreated to Ainneamh to await the arrival
of their guests. Symon had had a crowd of four—including himself.
But his parents and Hamil made up only a small fraction of all the
souls, powerful or not, who had come to witness Proìseil willingly,
or almost willingly, giving his daughter to a mage king.

He had chosen well indeed.

She whom he had chosen turned her lovely face up and smiled
at him. "Are you ready?"

"From the moment I saw you."

She laughed. "For me, as well."

"Will your sire survive the day, do you suppose?"

"He has softened toward you," she said. "He has, after all, prepared the wedding feast."

"I'll bid him taste my portion before I eat it," Symon said dryly,
but his heart was light as he said it. Perhaps 'twas a small thing, but
his marriage to Iolaire had opened up some bit of exchange between
Neroche and Ainneamh. He supposed that at some point in the
future that might be a boon in dealing with Lothar, should he find
himself free.

But that was far in the future and today was the day for other
beginnings. He took Iolaire's hand in his and walked with her
through that glittering hall to stand before the king of Ainneamh and
there claim her as his wife and queen. They passed the evening most
pleasantly in dancing and feasting. Symon glanced about him at one
point to find Ehrne engaged in conversation with Sgath and his wife
Eulasaid, the wizardess of Camanaë. Symon shook his head in silent

wonder. First it was Proìseil lowering himself to wed his daughter to a mage, then it was allowing his banished and subsequently quite teary-eyed brother to see his home again. Where would it end? The world no doubt held its breath...

Symon looked for his bride. Iolaire stood near her father, laughing with her younger brother and sister. Symon looked at her and marveled. She looked much as she had when he'd first looked upon her. She was dressed in a gown of hues that seemed to shift as she did; she still had that cascade of dark hair falling most of the way down her back, and her eyes were the same vivid blue. If there was grace, beauty, or goodness to be found anywhere in any of the Nine Kingdoms, it was in Ainneamh where Iolaire the Fair walked over green grass that never faded to brown —

Only now she was his and she was walking to him with a smile that was for him alone.

For a moment, he felt as if he were still in his father's winter retreat, making his own very short list of women he might want to wed and having but one name on it. He wondered if he would ever catch his breath from the wonder of being able to call that one name and have her answer as his.

"You are far away, my liege."

He shook his head. "I was thinking that you are like a whisper of spring in the middle of winter." He laughed, a little unsteadily. "I admit there are times I wonder if I will survive you."

She shook her head with a smile. "Nay, I will be winter's queen and happily so, for even in the quiet of the snow, we will have hope for the spring."

"Aye, there is that as well," he mused, feeling a deep peace sink into his heart.

And with that peace came a great joy in knowing that Iolaire would be his forever, her eternal springtime intertwining with the stillness of his winter kingdom.

"Come, my king," she said with a smile, "and let us celebrate while the evening lasts."

And so Symon, king of Neroche, took the hand of Iolaire, princess of Ainneamh, and walked into his future, clear-eyed and content.

About the Author

Lynn Kurland is the *New York Times* bestselling author of over forty novels and novellas. She can be reached through her website at www.LynnKurland.com.

Printed in Great Britain
by Amazon

25539941R00108